10694291

HADLEY

a novel by

Nick Macfie

HADLEY

ISBN-13: 978-988-19090-9-1

Hadley was written during Nick Macfie's tenure as a *Reuters* journalist, but *Reuters* has not been involved with the content or tone of this book, which are the author's responsibility alone.

This book has been reset in 10pt Book Antiqua. Spellings and punctuations are left as in the original edition.

HISTORY / Asia / China

EB025

Published by Earnshaw Books Ltd. (Hong Kong)

To Kyoung-yae, Emily and Hannah.
Special thanks to David Milnes and Hong Kong.

CHAPTER ONE

I STARED ACROSS Hong Kong harbour from my twenty-third floor office desk, squinting at the sun glinting off a sleek, white dinghy tacking to starboard to avoid a Star Ferry. A single cumulus cloud bobbed above the distant Lion Rock as a drill somewhere in the building pierced my head. A Lion Rock-sized hangover bobbed over my eyes, clouding my vision of the desk-top TV and my two computer screens.

My head was bobbing, my screens were bobbing. My whole life appeared to be bobbing. I pulled a waste-paper basket nearer with my foot, just in case the contents of my stomach bobbed. The noise came from above and below, dropping the lower-register sound of metal against concrete but taking on a shrill, constant, electronic, tropical-insect squeal. It didn't hurt my hangover – it *was* my hangover, penetrating from all sides and screaming through cupped hands: *When are you ever going to learn?*

Then it stopped.

"Thank you."

Da-ding, da-ding, da-ding. Just feet away, a school bell rang and rang. I made an "ooh" noise and buried my head in my palms. My news editor, a chirpy cockney called Rodney Baxter, squirming in a cream turtleneck jumper, was priming himself for an announcement, puffing his lips in and out. The bell dangled on a leather thong from his wrist, giving an occasional, muffled dong.

"Attention please!"

Never again, I thought. The incense-filled bars of Wanchai

could survive without me – for one night, anyway. On the TV news, a gorgeous Hong Kong celebrity who clearly had no business being on the news at all was saying anything that came into her head. "My body is unreasonably pleasurable," she was explaining. "It grooves and it curves and curves."

But it was an intense-looking old man leaning against a taxi and smirking behind her who made me wince and my heart groove and curve all by itself. The man sported a ponytail and an earring, his piercing eyes were looking straight at the TV camera. And straight at me.

"I know that man," I whispered. I looked round to see if anyone else in the room had noticed me talking to myself. Schoolboy butterflies passed through my stomach. Why? What was going on? The man wasn't paying any attention to the gorgeous girl. I swallowed. It was someone from years and years ago, back in England, but he wasn't English – that much I knew. And whoever it was, it was definitely *him*, not someone who looked like him. Someone sinister. A teacher? I could remember sinister teachers, but this guy wasn't one of them. Was it someone I interviewed on my first paper? Some ex-con who didn't like my court reporting? I turned down the sound but kept watching the man. The extraordinarily beautiful Canto pop star/actress kept talking at a thousand words a minute.

"Your attention *please!*" Clang, clang went the bell. I managed to look up, my head tilted to the left and seriously wounded. Next to my news editor, the chirpy Baxter, was someone who looked like Mao Zedong, or his widow. She even had a mole next to her nose.

"I want to introduce you all to Candy Kam," Baxter said.

The Candy Man Can. Singer and song writer Tony Newley. *Enough, enough.* I caught the gist of what Baxter was saying. Candy Kam was preparing the groundwork for a movie. It was to be about western journalists in the Exotic East and she needed colour. That meant real reporters, real lives, but also some of the mystery of the Exotic East. Baxter kept referring to the Exotic East. Why would anyone want to hear what western journalists thought about the Exotic East? They knew nothing about it – Baxter least of all. The man on the television frowned as he examined his nails. Who was this guy?

I know you, I thought.

"Don't be afraid to be stars," Candy said. "I think you are all handsomest."

The assembled journos, only two of whom had done any real reporting in the last twenty years, did not register her comments. By any stretch of the imagination, none of them could be described as handsome. Butt-ugly would be cruel but it would be closer.

I worked for Shrubs News Agency and the Asia-Pacific hub was the sleek office to which under-paid reporters from Afghanistan to New Zealand sent their stories. It was a hive of activity. Squabbling TV producers, overweight picture editors and, in my section, fifteen scruffy but colourfully dressed sub-editors who were meant to rewrite stories if necessary, question the sourcing, sharpen the first paragraph, add context, hone everything down and, with a touch of a button, send them to newspapers, TV and radio stations, banks and big-time investors across the world.

I lifted my head from my hands slowly to survey my section of the hive. An old Scottish sub known only as Fagin was reading the instructions of the popcorn machine which sat on his desk. A Canadian sub, talking to himself, was spraying blue paint on to what looked like a marijuana plant. An Englishman, Rupert, hands in pockets, was looking at the ceiling, humming and shaking his legs violently.

"Candy is looking for real-life journalists to play parts in the film," Baxter said. "Real life. She's particularly interested in anyone who's been in the Exotic East for a while."

The TV news had finished and the man leaning against the taxi had gone. A game show had begun. My whole life felt like a game show.

"You are all my material," Candy said. "Please behave."

Someone dug me in the ribs: "Opportunity knocks, old timer."

Old timer. Thanks for that. An old timer behaving in the Exotic East. What could be less exotic than sitting at a desk and subbing? Subbing was short for sub-editing and from time to time involved bouts of sobbing. The work could be remarkably pedantic and many would say it was the most boring job in journalism, the equivalent of being a linesman at a football match, ticking people off with a smile on your face, afraid of abuse. Watching life go by from the sidelines, but every now and then managing to attract everyone's attention by making a bad decision. Exotic was not a word usually associated with the Shrubs Asia-Pacific desk.

But the desk job meant I had regular shifts and regular hours to spend in the bars feeling sorry for myself at the grand old age of thirty-nine. My career, I would tell the girls, stretching self-indulgence across the harbour and back, was no longer brilliant. Now the girls had begun to ask: Well, when was it, Hadley? Never mind that now. Never mind brilliance. A mystery, a new game, had begun. I was being stalked by a man in his sixties.

Two days after seeing the man on the news, I took a packed Star Ferry from the main island of Hong Kong to the Kowloon peninsula. Tourists leant over the railings, dodging the plastic storm sheets and bashing their camcorders into one another as they zoomed in on the harbour, a passing fire boat, a picturesque junk with a fake sail, the looming, green Peak which looked down on the business district of Central. Six or seven adults were zooming and snapping away. At the stern, a man with a ponytail was facing inwards and his camcorder was trained on me. An instant later, he had turned and was pointing the camera at the Convention and Exhibition Centre.

The building looked like a Sydney Opera House that someone had gently crushed with the palm of his or her hand. I did not move and by the time the ferry had reached Kowloon-side, the man had disappeared into the crowds. That same night, I saw him on one of the matchbox-shaped trams which ran the length of the island, skirting the Wanchai bar district. The man, clearly a public transportation buff, was standing in the packed aisle a few rows in front of me, tapping the low roof with a newspaper and whistling a Burt Bacharach song, bending to look out of the open window. On closer inspection, he was definitely in his sixties, and looked alert. On the prowl. I felt sure he was someone I had met on my first newspaper in the flat, sugar-beet growing Fens in eastern England. I tried to push through the packed commuters but was too late: the man escaped into the crowd and the tram set off again with a nice, familiar "ding ding" of its bell.

The South China Morning Post, which I considered the most exotic masthead in the business, ran a Sunday feature about a movie which was to be directed by Adolf Lee, famous in Hong Kong for a string of low-budget kung fu flicks. Adolf had also directed a couple of recent hits in the West including 'Don't Be Cruel', the story of a Chinese Elvis impersonator who lived in Birmingham, Alabama. The other was 'Burt the Bellhop', a slow, black and white film about a California hotel seen through the eyes of a bearded bellhop from Canada. With a couple more large Black Labels inside me than the co-pilot, I had seen the tail end of 'Burt the Bellhop' on a plane. It was awful. The Post said there was speculation about a number of actors playing the lead part of the foreign correspondent, including Sean Connery, who was way too old for it – but then they had hauled in Michael Caine to play the journo in 'The Quiet American' a few years back and he was close to seventy at the time. Nothing about the story was known, but the venture already had clout. The working title was 'I Love Hong Kong', which also happened to be the slogan of one of the local political parties.

The paper said the press speculation was off the mark and

that the film, according to inside sources (as opposed to outside sources who knew nothing about it) would most probably star Hong Kong's own Panda Koo, the very same celebrity on the television talking about her pleasurable body, acting alongside 'up-and-coming young British actor Chris Torment'.

The whisky I was drinking as I read this at my local bar shot out of my nose. The pain was overwhelming. I was sitting at the Honest Bar in Kam Tin, in Hong Kong's still partly rural New Territories on the far side of Lion Rock. It was surrounded by croaking frogs and duck farms pouring shit into streams and car-wrecking yards leaking battery acid. I scowled as I dabbed my nostrils with a beer mat.

I had been at school with Torment in England – Halfords, a grim, second-rate public school on the boggiest and windiest side of Sotobech in the Fens. At school, Torment had wanted to be an actor. He had also wanted to be a commando. He had an artistic and military bent and he used to beat the shit out of me. Maria, a long-legged Filipina in cut-off jeans and the star of the Honest Bar, sat painting her toenails behind the counter. Her bottom was like an apple. She listened to my ear, nose and throat outburst.

"You eat shit and die, Hadley. Why you making a noise like an elephant?"

"I'm sorry. Went down the wrong way. Lordy, lordy."

Eat shit and die was a term of endearment. Not the title of a book about punctuation.

"You drink too much and your face flushes."

"Yes, I'm sorry."

"Well, stop."

I LAY ON THE FLOOR of my office, studying the underside of my boss's rosewood desk, at the end of a hard late shift and a few hours on the town. I had slept there many times, but never allowed myself the time to have a good look, and I despaired at what little effort had been put into making a piece of furniture which from afar looked terrific and from up close smelt nice. The red varnish, which covered the swirling dragons and Chinese characters on the top and front, came to an abrupt halt where the 'sifu' master carpenter had assumed that no one would bother to look. The rosewood had switched to a two-ply affair with pencil scribbling, arrows and a nasty smear which looked like blood. I tapped the wood, avoiding nails that no one had bothered hammering in. It made a thin, hollow noise – not surprising, as it was the underside of a drawer, but it was tacky and carelessly made nevertheless. It was a bit like the news agency, doing things on the cheap because it thought no one would take a closer look. I turned my head on my briefcase and studied the woodwork again, the bit that went down next to the knee. More smears of blood (what went *on* under here?).

"You awake, Hadley?"

I turned my head to the light. I saw A4 paper folding on to the floor from two noisy, old-fashioned printers. There were coffee stains on the patches of grey carpet which, like stripes on a lawn, were exaggerated by being viewed at ground level.

"Nurse?"

"No nurse here," said ah-Jeung, the copy girl. "All nurses in hospital busy giving injections and doing good works."

I twisted my neck as much as it could stand and saw the television screen showing an old black-and-white Cantonese movie.

"Hadley, you awake?"

"What's the matter? You've got a story?"

"You say to wake you, to watch CNN and the BBC. But you always sleep."

I climbed up from the floor and stretched. "And why you wear such clothes?" ah-Jeung asked.

I looked down and frowned. I was wearing white cricket flannels with a red stain down the side of the crotch.

"Why you have big red mark?" ah-Jeung asked.

I didn't have a clue. "These aren't my trousers," I said gormlessly. "These are cricket trousers. I don't understand."

"But why you have big red mark? Right in the front?"

"It's where you rub the ball... well, not you." I swore to myself I would clean up my life. Become a responsible veteran wire reporter. "It's where the bowler rubs the ball. Shines it on one side... It's very difficult to explain in non-cricketing terms."

"What's non-cricketing mean? I think you drink too much beer. I think you are a little bit alcoholic."

The trousers were a mystery. I tried to retrace my steps since leaving the office, a stone's throw away from velvety girlie bars and sleaze, at about midnight wearing a respectable pair of blue Marks & Spencer chinos. Something along the way had made me decide to abandon the trousers in favour of a pair of cricket flannels with a red stain down the crotch. I looked again at the stain. It was the colour of lipstick. Now I was really frowning. Memories clicked in, one by one, but nothing untoward. The usual banter with the girls, making the mama-sans laugh, the smell of incense in the doorways and of cheap but nice perfume out back, the wet tile floors and the cramped men's room, the smell of fried tofu coming through the vent. I was at ease at the long bars, buying the girls shots of Sprite at 250 times the rate in the real world outside.

"You so sweet, Hadley. You so nice," the girls said.

"You bar-fine me, Hadley. Mama give you a good price. I make you feel good."

But I couldn't really afford to bar-fine them. Across the street, a stooped Chinese woman with jagged teeth tried to get me up a flight of dark concrete steps. Not for the first time. What *for*? I knew what for. But who in their right mind would consider the option? The women standing around waiting for their prey, once snared by the old crone with the teeth, were all pushing sixty. Under a dim, naked bulb, the concrete steps rose steeply into blackness, oblivion. To go up there alone would be foolhardy, but with an eighty-year-old bag or one of her middle-aged good-time girls? Who would do it?

A British detective, for one. He was a surly regular on the strip and we were on nodding terms. I had walked on two steps after fending off the crone when I heard her accost someone else. I turned and saw the officer of the law, his head hung low, walking up the stairs to negotiate some nodding terms of his own.

Escorted by a woman in front and behind, both with a sudden spring in their step, he looked like he was being led to the guillotine. If the ancient woman's teeth were anything to go by, the guillotine was not far off the mark.

"Hadley!"

"Yes. Okay."

I tried to watch the news. I hadn't touched a cricket bat in thirty years and I didn't know anyone who played cricket. That was my point. What had happened to my trousers?

I sat at my desk and switched on the screens. Bangladesh had filed an overnight update to a ferry disaster. As ever, tragic and bizarre. I groaned. Never mind the trousers. Bangladesh copy would do it every time.

The reporters in Dhaka were always being reminded by the desk to weave in background and put everything into context. Assume the reader knows nothing about Bangladesh. Make him want to read on. Fat chance. The subs read on in Bangladesh stories just to see how and where the background – always cut and pasted from previous stories – was sloshed in like wet cement. More often than not, it was in a quote. The story on my screen was no exception:

"Two overcrowded ferries collided early on Friday on an enormously mighty river in Bangladesh killing at least 100 people, police and survivors said.

"'It is terrible,' said one woman in the water after the enormous and mighty collidings. 'I blame the huge and mighty river, which winds through this impoverished, flood-prone country of 147 million people

and opens into the sea at the major port of Chittagong, 130 miles south-east of the capital Dhaka.'"

My first act of malice was to insert 'poverty-stricken' in front of 'Bangladesh' (at the same time thinking that even when I did play cricket, I was never a bowler). My second act was to slip in the words 'basket case'. Then I spiked the bloody thing and had a cigarette on the fire stairs. I was considering quitting my job and branching out into something new and useful, when the answer to the most important question of all raced back like a cocker spaniel with a sloppy ball. The answer to a crossword clue comes when you stop thinking about it. The best headline ('laughing all the way to the banquet', a night earlier, about China's new and burgeoning middle class) comes when you are working on another story.

The man with the ponytail – I had finally placed him. And there he was again, on the television. The same clip of the gorgeous Panda Koo being repeated.

"Ah-Jeung, turn that back."

"Ah? Turn what back? This is TV, no tape."

"But that man..."

"What man?"

I strode forward and tapped the television. "That man. He's American and I know him. Why is he smirking at me?"

Ah-Jeung responded in fast, impatient Cantonese.

"I know him now," I said, sitting down. My heart was beating way too fast for someone whose only exercise was bar hopping and smoking two packets of cigarettes a day. At seven in the morning I was wearing flannels with a big red stain and, my eyes closed, was thinking about the man on TV who was giving my head the spins.

It was Joe. Joe the American.

I had never known his other name. I had met him on my first newspaper, the Sotobech Sentinel, back in the sodden Fens twenty-odd years earlier. The news story at the time was a remake of

'Great Expectations', Chris Torment's first movie, which wasn't a story at all. There was no one famous in it and I had struggled to find my peg – until I saw some spectators, all wearing dark suits, sitting in, or leaning against, three black Cadillacs. Away from the tilting Portaloos, mini-vans, buzzing transformers and boxy, upright 1980s English caravans, all in a haze of the smoke of fried onions, there was a bunch of guys who looked threatening and undoubtedly American.

Joe had been part of the group and was monitoring the film shoot, looking alert and intense, just as he did now. I had approached the men and asked them about the film and ended up being invited to Joe's house to watch a James Bond movie with the other men in suits, at least one of whom was wearing a shoulder holster... The details were no longer clear.

I left the office the next night and crossed the road to the Rawhide Club, where the velvet walls were draped with whips and studded with gunbelts and cartwheels.

"Hadley! You come back!"

Three Filipinas, wearing sweaters over their bikinis, skipped over to the front door end of the bar, eager for their Sprite fix.

"Hey there, girls." I saw the detective from the night before, sitting alone in the middle of the bar and staring at his drink. What romantic interlude lies in store for you tonight, detective, here in the Exotic East? What stairway to a particularly murky heaven awaits you? The detective turned slowly towards me and nodded. I smiled and nodded back as I downed a San Miguel which had appeared without my having to order it. This was my quality time. A Thai girl approached, efforts of a smile on a beautiful face which I stretched out to touch – and then I froze.

"Hadley? Hadley, what's wrong?"

Behind the beautiful Thai, behind the nodding detective, sitting at the far end of the bar next to one of the VIP sofas and tables discreetly hidden behind plastic foliage, was the man with the ponytail.

"Hadley? You've gone all red."

"It's okay," I said. "I have to..."

What did I have to do? What had I done to warrant this attention? (Was it the trousers?) The man was stalking me day and night. I said my apologies to the Thai girl and walked the length of the bar, past the detective, to Joe's stool. I studied the profile and the man ignored me. It was a smiling face now, self-conscious. One second there was a lot of hand movement, rubbing of the jaw and the cheeks, and then he was still. I felt my heart do one of its unhealthy skips.

"Do you remember me?"

Joe, the American movie man, turned and smiled. He looked like an overweight boxer with hairs on his nose.

"No. I don't think so."

He turned back to the bar. I stared some more and Joe was smirking again. A lot of neck movements now, like a hen, as he studied a photo of Clint Eastwood as Rowdy Yates on the wall in front of him.

"But I remember you. I remember you from Sotobech."

"You don't know me from Adam, pal."

"No, but I do. You mustn't mess me around. I met you in Sotobech when they were filming 'Great Expectations'. I came to your house."

Joe turned and looked at me. Never one for reflection, I thought back briefly to the Fens and remembered 'Cadillac' written on the wing mirror of one of the limos. Almost twenty years earlier.

" 'Great Expectations'? I know that movie," Joe said, looking me up and down, his eyes resting briefly on the red stain next to my crotch. "David Lean, 1946. Class act."

"No, not that one. They were doing a remake. And you and your friends were there. Driving Cadillacs."

Joe drummed his fingers on the bar. He caught the eye of the Thai girl and winked. " 'Great Expectations', you say. Funny, I've never seen it. Maybe they never got around to making it. Have you seen it?"

"No, but..."

"They say seeing is believing. I reckon they didn't make it in the end. I reckon they came to their senses, out there on that God-forsaken swamp, and gave up the whole shooting match."

"So you do remember?"

Joe slapped his hand on the bar and got up from the stool. He looked at me and sighed.

"I'll be seeing you," he said, brushing ash off my shoulder. "We can talk more about the movies. Big James Bond fan myself."

Joe started down the aisle to the door and turned, a smile on his face.

"Tip of the day," he said. "Don't be so scared. Take a risk here and there. Nice pants, by the way."

And with that, he was out through the velvet curtains into the neon light and road-side incense. I asked the mama-san if she had seen Joe before. She said he was a first-time cheap Charlie.

CHAPTER TWO

I WAS CALLED, apparently on Candy Kam's recommendation, to audition for a speaking part in the Hong Kong movie – a movie that I was convinced Joe was involved in up to his jiggling hen's neck. Not only did Candy want me to audition, she also wanted some of the film crew to come round to my office to see how I spent the day.

"We need to catch you in your full action," she had said.

Action? Ha! I had done some real reporting for Shrubs, boarding planes to neighbouring trouble spots. I had even been held by little known rebels in the Philippines who spent their spare time running through Eagles songs on acoustic guitars. I was amazed at how often my intros, or first paragraphs, would be, or could be, the same as those I had written on the Sotobech Sentinel. I had been sent to Pakistan, Afghanistan, Indonesia and South Korea, but I hadn't done much reporting in Hong Kong.

No one had told Candy that there was a Hong Kong Shrubs reporting bureau, on the same floor as the Asia-Pacific desk, in which there were real reporters who did things like go out and meet people. They had accessories – digital recorders, fancy phones. They said things like "let's take this offline" and "let's think outside the box and when we've done that, let's do lunch". I hadn't done lunch with anyone in close to fifteen years, but managed to turn up for the audition at the Wanchai Arts Centre at 2 p.m. on the nose. I was wearing a grey tee-shirt, grey jacket and grey trousers. I had also put mousse on my untidy hair, which made it look slightly grey. Candy met me in the foyer and led me through to the Lion Dance Practice Room. She took a seat behind a desk where two Western women were shuffling notes.

"You're welcome," Candy said inappropriately, motioning me towards a chair. My village house was about the same size as a dentist's waiting room and I was not used to so much uncluttered space.

"Mr Arnold," said the woman in the middle. She was American, bookish, mid-40s and wearing glasses. "Welcome to this audition."

"Thank you very much. I want to thank…"

"My name is Gretel. Candy you already know."

She didn't introduce the woman at the end of the desk, who was dark and hard and fiddling with a video camera on a scarred tripod.

"Thank you."

"I am the co-producer," Gretel said. "We are going to ask you some questions which you will answer to camera. First I would like you to give this a quick read." She gave me a page of script. "Until you are familiar with it. And then, as naturally as you can, give it to camera. How do you feel?"

As Gretel spoke, her face expanded into a wide smile which would switch back into a grimace. Like Condoleezza Rice. Or Margaret Thatcher.

"I know Chris Torment," I said.

"Oh really. He's a fine actor." Gretel stared at me.

"Oh really." I stared. "I also know Joe."

"Joe?"

"Joe. Yes."

"Mr Arnold…"

"Hadley."

"Hadley, we must move this along."

"I understand."

"Okay, I suggest you don't try to memorise the lines. Familiarise yourself with them, use them as a prompt, then talk to us. Talk to the three of us as if you were in the Foreign Correspondents' Club with your colleagues. Ad-lib. Be as natural as you can. Please go ahead. You are Philip."

I put Joe to one side as if he were of no importance and looked at the script. What I said when I was in the FCC with my colleagues bore no resemblance to this. It seemed... extraordinary.

I frowned as I read:

MAGNUS

So Philip, how's that young filly of yours?

PHILIP

Not too shabby actually.

MAGNUS

That's good. Because I was wondering how
she was. Captain, can we have some more
drinks here? A pink gin and the usual. Actually, Philip, the reason I asked you here
this evening is because of the riots. You
know the scene. What's going on?

PHILIP

Oh, Magnus, how much time have you got?
The riots. What a mess. It's going to get
bloody, that's for sure. Talk to me about
riots. The Chinamen think they've got us on
the run. They don't know what we're made
of. The Yanks think we're limeys. I'm not
so sure.

And there it ended. I was shocked. I gave a little cough. "I'm sorry. This is part of the film?"

"We're still writing it. We're making it up as we go along. Consider this just your audition part."

"You want me to do it now?" I had started sweating. Never a good sign.

"In your own time. No need to memorise it. Use it as a prompt. You're in the FCC with your colleagues."

"You be a star," Candy added. It was pure, affectionate encouragement. "You're welcome."

"It's just that I've never called anyone a Chinaman in my life. I don't want to sound self-righteous, but I don't know anyone who has. And I think pink gin went out of fashion around the time of the first opium war. But it sounds good. Gin with a splash of Angostura bitters, right?"

"Never mind the pink gin. It's a prompt."

"Has Joe seen this?"

"Joe?"

"Yes. Has he seen this? I doubt he would give his approval, if he were being forthright." I took off a pair of grey-tinted sunglasses. "He seems a forthright sort of person, don't you think?"

"I don't know Joe. We must move on."

"It's just that this conversation is strange. Hong Kong is not like this."

The woman at the end of the desk raised the camera. I spent a few moments with the lines. I tried to feel them and managed to put Joe out of my mind. Again. Magnus and Philip, they were the ones to worry about here. Who were these guys? This was a crossroads. The movie world, with open arms, awaits at the end of this audition. Just don't mess it up. Remember what your English teacher said when you were playing Queen Anne with the pointy hat and long billowing gown and the fags in your pocket. Don't gobble your words. Let hump-backed Richard III woo you. Relax. I was thinking of what Gretel had said. Improvise. You are at the FCC now. You are speaking to three colleagues, and you're talking about those riots licking at the door of the club, gathering steam on Ice House Street outside. You can see clubs and rude banners waving outside the window. Terms of abuse. What are you, as Philip, saying? I took a deep breath and looked at Candy. I paused several seconds. And then:

"Bugger me, the riots!"

This was a bellow. Candy shot back in her chair, scraping the floor. She almost fell over. I had shot my bolt. I had nothing more. There was a long pause.

"Um, don't talk to me about them," I whispered, rising fast to another bellow. It was coming back. I had to ad-lib. Just slow down a bit. "You guys, you think you're limeys. But what do you know. You're... you're shabby. Actually, you and your fillies."

I turned along the line to the woman holding the camera which appeared to be rocking. I pursued the ad-libbing. I was in the FCC.

"Look at me when I'm talking to you." Where did the northern accent come from? It was some Yorkshire comedian from my youth. Never mind that now. "I said look at me when I'm talking to you! You... yank." Change the pace. Show your versatility, your range of emotion. I turned back to Candy, leant forward, looked down at my wringing hands and then up at Candy's horrified face.

"How long have you been in this town?" I asked.

"But... but I was born..."

Gretel hushed her up. I had them in the palm of my hand. This movie business was a cinch.

"Four months?" I asked incredulously. "Four *months*? I've been in this town fifteen years. I know these people. Who do you know?" My shoulders were shrugged, my arms were stretched. "Don't talk to me about taxis. Don't give me your pink gins. You drink pink gin? You do? I'll tell you what you are. You're nothing less than... an arse. What do you say to that? Ah? Ah?"

I put my hand to my ear (a lovely touch) and ended with a mocking: "I can't hear you."

I sat back triumphantly. I had strayed from the script, it was true, but I was letting it all out. It was natural – I was a natural. I looked at Gretel who in turn was staring back with her mouth open. She's speechless, I thought. She certainly didn't say anything. None of them did for a while.

"I think that's what you call a wrap," I said.

"It was certainly very expressive," Gretel said. The woman with the camera was making noises into a handkerchief.

"I can do some more, if you'd like."

"No, please. That was exactly the right length."

Candy stretched out a hand to me and said: "You are terrorist."

"Mr Arnold," Gretel said. "That was just fine."

Now that was a coincidence. Because when I did my Jimmy Stewart impression, in the bar after a few eye-openers, that was the line I used. "Well that's just fine." To be sure, this appeared to be an omen.

"Now. If you're ready, we'd like you to answer some questions. Into the camera."

"Fire away."

"I'm sorry." The woman with the camera left the room. Why did she have to run?

Gretel read from a sheet of paper. "Could you tell us, in your own words, of some experience in Hong Kong which reflects the city and your feelings for it?" She looked up. "A relationship, perhaps. An encounter with a local girl. Some first impressions."

Now this really was a good omen. Why would they ask for more if they hadn't liked the acting? They like what they have seen so far. Candy was behind the camera now. I swung my eyes moodily towards her.

"On my first day, I checked in at an old hotel in Wanchai," I said. "The Luk Kwok – Six Countries – you'd know it, it was in the Suzie Wong movie. It was knocked down years ago and has since been rebuilt. Anyway, I'd checked in. A small room. The first thing I noticed was the damp, the smell of damp. It was everywhere in those days. Newspapers were delivered in cellophane. Stamps you glued on yourself in the post office, otherwise they'd stick to anything."

Was this really interesting? I wondered.

"I'd bought an alarm clock which would turn itself off at any sound. The alarm, that is. In those days that was new. You could shout at it in the morning and if would turn itself off. I was sitting in my room trying to get it to work. But I couldn't make it ring. You know why? The air-conditioner. The air-conditioning was so loud, it was turning off the alarm before it had a chance to make a noise! There was nothing wrong with the clock. In fact I still have it. Made in Germany. The joke is, or was, that the air-conditioner was loud, and yet the room was so damp. These days you don't hear the air-conditioning, yet your room's freezing and there's no damp!"

Gretel's eyes had glazed over. "Wow," she said, allowing herself a little chuckle. I joined her. "Well, this is just fine, Mr Arnold. Just fine. But we were wondering about more personal experiences. The clash of cultures. Hong Kong love, perhaps."

"Yes, yes. To be sure. I'll get to that. Anyway, the next morning, here I was in the heart of the city. I was woken up by a cock. Not an alarm clock! A cock crowing in the heart of the city! It was March, like now, and dark clouds hung over the hills and I felt completely alive. This was the other side of the world to me. I was in my twenties and I felt reborn. I strode out of the front door on to the street, stood on the pavement, and stretched my arms in the air with a big smile on my face. I felt a new beginning. There was a man standing next to me, an old Chinese guy looking the other way, waiting for a bus. He turned in one swift movement and gobbed down my trousers."

"Gobbed?"

"Gobbed. Spat." I made the noise. "All down my trousers. But the funny thing was, I wasn't angry. I'm English. I may have apologised. But I was surprised. And so was the old Chinese guy. You know, the old Chinaman. He leapt into the air and said something I didn't understand. I looked down and saw the gob on my khaki trousers. Just then the old man reached down and tried to wipe it away. He was elongating the stain. He was elongating it. It was now about seven inches long and sticking to my knee."

"Seven inches? What did you do?"

"I changed my trousers."

"No. I mean before that."

"I can't remember."

"Did you hit him? Or start shouting?"

"No."

"You didn't call the police?"

"No. It was an accident. He was trying to clean it up."

Candy was keen to be heard. "Did you yell, screaming 'police, police'?"

"No. I don't remember that. The point is, I was on top of the world. I was on the other side of the world. People gob in this town, more loudly and carelessly than this guy. He just happened to hit me. If he hadn't hit me, it would have gone in the gutter. I wasn't angry. I was just part of what happened. Spitting isn't meant to be offensive. It *can* be meant to be offensive, but generally it isn't. Well, it is in Beijing sometimes. But that's another story. It's very cold in Beijing."

"Okay, let's move along. What about the love? The girls, I mean."

I was now completely at ease. And expansive.

"Imagine, if you will, Wanchai without the towers. Without the hotels you're staying in. Imagine a street lined with bars, without the Filipinas and Thais you see today. There are scores, I mean scores, of Chinese girls. Actually, mostly women. Older women. Wearing blowsy ballroom gowns, billowing gowns, and huddled together, well past their sell-by date."

Sell-by date. I hadn't used language like that in years. But this was the movies.

"Imagine, at the end of the strip, next to an English-style pub packed at 5 a.m. with Triads and suits who can't bear to go home to their wives. Imagine a bar called the Mermaid. Black curtains at the front. Inside, a long bar with just enough room for bar stools. At the end an altar to a bright and painted god, stuffed with incense sticks, oranges and monopoly money. Personalised match boxes, black and purple, with a picture of a mermaid sitting in a glass of champagne. These are details."

"Very sad," said Candy.

"No. Not very sad. Just…"

"No, please. Very sad. You are adult man. You like Hong Kong as British colony, but Hong Kong always part of China. No more like this."

Candy was wrong. Hong Kong hadn't changed. The bars stayed open until daylight arrived along with the clang and growl of the trams, the steam from the dim sum stalls and the newspapers delivered to street hawkers piled high on the backs of bicycles. This time of day was too late for tourists, except for the repeat visitors who came each year for the cricket sixes and rugby sevens, recidivists at sixes and sevens, on which days I would avoid the strip altogether. I was also put off by the swaggering U.S. Navy, who once a month would overload the bars, drink a lot and be disarmingly nice. When the Yanks were in town, with their heaving chants in the clubs – "East Coast! East Coast!, West Coast! West Coast!" – I found refuge at the Honest Bar. It was the lone survivor on Kam Tin's own Suzie Wong strip, joined by a string of coloured lights, which had thrived in May's day thanks to the nearby British garrison. The soldiers had gone, the barracks, block after block, stood empty. May, a young Cantonese girl who had always smiled when she saw me, had also gone. Village schools in Nissen huts, corner shops, car parking spaces marked 'mums only', had all been abandoned. Most of the Kam Tin bars had closed because of the drop in business and the rest were burnt down by Triads, according to the local press. Around the corner from the Honest Bar was a sixteenth century Chinese village fort with stone walls eighteen inches thick, and everyone who lived behind them had the same name.

I was on my fifth large Black Label and flushed. I was sitting at the bar, staring at myself in the dance floor mirror (never one for reflection ha ha) which had sprigs of plastic holly around the edge from Christmases past. I recalled the audition that afternoon and tried to sum it up in one word.

"Fuck."

At the side of the dance floor was a pile of boxes of Carlsberg and next to them, propped up against the wall, was a dusty Remington typewriter. It had been there for as long as I could remember.

"Maria, Maria, don't be so contrary."

"You give me a part in your film, I'll be hospitalised."

"Hospitable."

"Why, what's wrong?"

"What?"

I flashed back again to the audition and shuddered. That script. That northern accent. And what bloody riots?

"It'll begin with a panoramic sweep of the harbour, with a voiceover," I said. "No. Worse than that. It'll be a sweep of the bars in Wanchai, with the same voiceover."

"What's a voiceover?"

"Him. Torment. He'll be saying: 'Her name was May', spoken low and rising, as if you were talking to a girl who'd locked herself inside a cupboard."

What had happened to May, I wondered again. Always sitting with her straight back, so polite and charging so much money to go home with grey, ghostly customers – much more than any of the other girls. And then, as she was passing through the velvet curtains behind some overweight, middle-aged suit, there would always be that last glance over her shoulder and a bright smile and flash of the eye-lids for me. Every time. *Every* time. And I would repay it with a weak, remorseful wince, sitting still at the bar and ordering another drink. A bright smile one way, almost a scowl the other. Hopeless. I had asked mama-sans about her again and again over the years and they had just shrugged their shoulders.

"Who's May?" Maria asked. "What are they doing in a cupboard?"

"No one's in the cupboard. It's just the way you say the name. Low and rising. He'll say: 'She had long, straight hair. On the Star Ferry. Of an evening. And she was the most beautiful girl he'd ever seen.' Dear oh dear."

"Do you go in the cupboard?"

"I expect so. But the point is, Maria – the point is, this film is going to be woeful."

"No, you are going to be this word. You are going to be in it, right?"

"Yes, yes. Maybe. I gave so much of myself. My inner self. But there's a limit to what I can do. To save it. To save it from itself."

"What's the story?"

"I don't believe they know, Maria, to tell you the truth."

"You don't know truth. You lazy bullshit."

"May will probably be in it. At least Torment will think it's May. But it won't be May. Listen to this. It will be her twisting twin from China!"

"Shut up."

"And he's never met him. Her."

"Who's never met her?"

"She's never met him. Because he had an incurable disease! But the man, this bully of a man, while he was fighting off the Triads, in the riots, the third that day, lost his notebook and banged his head in the FCC and got his memory back. And he remembered that before Magnus became a shit-hot foreign correspondent, he got a first class degree in tropical medicine. He remembers the Quad, the windy cloisters, the echoes in the studies. And he recognizes the symptoms!"

"It sounds exciting," said ah-Fei, the sixty-year-old manager who hated me like he hated all loud, red-faced gweilos.

"It sounds bullshit," Maria said. "That's that movie 'Tootsie.' You piece of shit. You're copying all your shit and bringing it in here."

"Maria?"

"What?"

"You're beautiful."

For twenty-eight-year-old Maria, it must be pointed out, language was her first line of defence to fend off wandering hands and affections, a trick she had picked up as a young girl in Manila. But she found it difficult to distinguish between the customers, especially in her Wanchai days, so she used bad language all the time. She saved the worst for me.

I was panting. I pointed at Maria and squinted like Bill Clinton.

"I can name, and I can bet money on it, eight, no less than eight, stars of that movie. Tell me I can't."

"Who cares?"

"Eight. No more, no less."

"You piece of shit. Dustin Hoffman."

I raised my hand and counted off one on my thumb.

"That's one. Go on."

"What do you mean go on? You're the one who said he could name these people. Now you ask me. John Travolta."

"John Travolta? What's the matter with you?"

"Dustin Hoffman," said a man taking a seat at the end of the bar, a cigar clamped between his teeth. "Jessica Lange, Charles Durning, Geena Davis, Dabney Coleman, Teri Garr, Bill Murray. How many is that? Sydney Pollack. That should do it."

I realized my mouth was hanging slightly open and gently twisted, as if I had suffered a stroke. I stared at Joe but had nothing to say. I realised I had not stopped thinking about Joe, lingering somewhere in the back of my mind, since he had reappeared in my life. I also realised that I had been followed for more than just a few days and wondered about the likelihood of the relationship ending in violence.

"Who are you?"

"John Travolta was nowhere near that film, thank God," Joe said, putting his hand out to Maria. "Hi, I'm Joe."

I watched them shake hands. This man isn't interested in you, Maria, I thought. He isn't staring at your legs or at your bum. He is only interested in me. He has come all the way out into the New Territories, off the tourist track, to see me. He is a strange, and possibly dangerous, dingbat.

"Maria, I don't know who this is, or what he is doing here, or why he is following me around town."

"Yeah, right. In your dreams, shit-for-brains." Maria turned away.

"So I guess she does a lot of church work, this Maria?" Joe said. "Flower arrangements, meals on wheels, that kind of thing? Maybe the occasional movie review for the Christian Science Monitor?"

"Why are you following me?" I asked.

"Hadley and I met a long time ago," Joe said, raising his voice in Maria's direction. "He was a reporter on a local paper back in England. He liked my car. An American car. He thought there was a story in it."

"Hadley's a piece of shit." Maria said.

"I wouldn't go that far, my dear."

"I thought you were film producers," I said.

"Right."

"And you said you weren't."

"Your memory is very good," Joe said, looking at Maria, who lifted her eyes skywards and walked away. "She's a pretty girl. Make someone a fine wife. I can see you two have a thing. Don't be so English. I hope she isn't doing middle-aged men for money. No offence."

"Is that what you've come here to say?"

Joe dipped his head, a gesture I immediately remembered from the house near the silk farm in the Fens, and frowned. Joe was animated but sober. A scar, which I assumed was from an attack, not an operation, ran down the side of his neck. I slowly put my drink on the bar, trying to control a slight shake in my hand.

"I don't mean to be self-righteous," Joe said. "Because if you were to change your mind, she's a pretty little thing. I could easily court her myself."

"Court her? What kind of language is that? You must be seventy."

"Woo her. Win her over. I know I'm not as young as I used to be, but I can still turn a few heads. It's the demeanour and the confidence, something you know nothing about, which is why you've turned from that nice, fresh-faced, inquisitive young man into an old grouch. I'm here because I need your help. Sorry about all the cloak and dagger stuff. I was just sizing you up."

"How do you need my help? Why? The last time I saw you was twenty years ago."

"But we never forget, you see. Our firm. We take notes and we follow up on things. We see jobs through."

"Well I see through you. I'm going now. Really great catching up after all these years."

Joe stood up. "Same here. Good to see you again. Here's my card."

I looked at the inscription.

GUARDIAN CONTRACTS INC

JOE STEIN

MANAGER, ASIA/PACIFIC

"What are guardian contracts?"

"Nothing you will find online. We can talk later. Call me. Now you're in the movies, and knowing how much you like the movies, I am sure you can help me."

"I'm not in the movies. I've just had an audition for a bit part. And you are a disturbance."

"You're in the movies," Joe said. "That's why I'm here. I've got to go. But just want to give you some advice. Tip of the day: hold back that hostility. For now. You can put it to good use later. We'll get together soon."

CHAPTER THREE

WHEN I STARTED out in the newspaper business back in the Fens, I was struck by an ailment. The symptoms were yawning lapses in concentration. Black holes which could be measured by minutes or hours and which generally destroyed the job at hand. The problem surfaced in about my third week on the Sotobech Sentinel. I had gone to a parish council meeting in some god forsaken village made up of caravans and barns full of swedes, a revolting, mushy, orange vegetable that people only seem to eat at school. I was keeping pace with a councillor's complaints about dangerous dykes when my head turned to the window and my mind turned to a court reporter on a rival paper called Sabrina, who had textbook Pitman New Era shorthand, slender, piano-playing fingers and sumptuous red nails. Suddenly there was a huge commotion in the hall. The councillor, named Thomas, had sat down and fellow council members were banging their fists on the table shouting "shame, shame"... I hadn't a clue what was going on and there were no other reporters to ask for help. Certainly no Sabrina. When the meeting finished, the councillors were all so angry, no one would stop to explain what had happened. So it was left to me to call Mr Thomas himself the next morning to get some quotes and write up the story before I left for Wisbech Crown Court and the continuing case of the sulking Sotobech salesman stabbed with a sugar beet.

"Mr Thomas?"

"Dr. Thomas. This is he."

"Sorry. Doctor." (This is he?) "This is Hadley Arnold from the Sotobech Sentinel. I'm a new reporter here. I was at last night's parish council meeting and I was wondering if you would care to expand on the... business at hand as I am sure it would be of interest, of real importance, to our readers. After all you did stir up quite a commotion..."

I sat smiling, twiddling my pencil, confident of a great story unfolding. I was also aware of the news editor listening to the phone call. This made me nervous. There was silence on the other end of the line. Then:

"This is Dr. Thomas. This is he."

For some reason, I could not let on to my news editor that Thomas hadn't caught a word. I ruled out a re-introduction. I felt it would reflect on my abilities as a reporter, especially after not having got the story the night before and not having it written up ready for the news editor that morning. So instead of starting again more loudly, I plunged into an abyss.

"I see," I said, scrawling fictitious notes. "That's really interesting."

"Who is on the line? What's going on?"

"You don't say." I was writing "somebody please help me" in my notebook.

"Look, who is this? I warn you that I am a parish councillor and a magistrate."

"And so you're pushing ahead with your plans, then. When you've got the green light. Is that what you're saying?"

"You bastard."

"That's incredible."

"I'm hanging up now and may consider calling the police. Do you hear me?"

"Planning permission for a sugar loft and a beet liquidiser. With ancillary buildings. Good heavens, that's extraordinary."

My heart was beating fast. "No please, it's my pleasure. It was great meeting you last night, by the way."

"I'm doing it now. I tell you I'm furious. I'm hanging up now."

Another morning, I had set out for Stand Backwash Fen to cover the launch of an express bus service to Half Past Fen. The plan was to get on board and speak to passengers and hear them say what a boon this service was. It was called the Fen Express. I arrived with ten minutes to spare. I sat down and had a cup of tea with a Fen official who was explaining the timetable when I got to thinking about what a funny word "fen" was, and that the adjective, "fenny", if there was one, would be even funnier. I had started thinking about Fen and the Art of Motorcycle Maintenance, when I realised the Fen Express had left without me.

I jumped aboard another bus going in the same direction, hoping to board the Fen Express at its destination, Half Past Fen, but the Fen Express was so fast that my bus passed it heading back to Stand Backwash Fen. What a rush!

I managed to counter these lapses by trying to concentrate on what I saw, not what I heard. Filling in the colour. That was what I had been doing that time I met Joe. It all came back to me at my twenty-third floor desk in Hong Kong in the middle of a story about a man with no intestines climbing Mount Everest. I had to leave the room. My heart was beating furiously.

I took the lift down to the marbled foyer, paced up and down and lit a cigarette. The assignment, all those years ago, was the kind every reporter liked, except at that point in my career, I had never heard anyone on the weekly Sotobech Sentinel (circulation: twenty thousand) ever call them assignments. I had wandered leisurely around the 'Great Expectations' film set, my jacket hooked over my shoulder and notebook in hand. There was no hard news to worry about. It was a matter of walking around with a smile, nodding at people and saying "wotcha", trying not to trip over cables and keeping away from the stars, who were far too busy to talk to the press. Soak up the atmosphere, find a nice peg and write eight hundred easy words.

Precious few real stars appeared to be involved in 'Great Expectations', but it was of interest to Sotobech readers because it was happening on their patch and the actor playing Pip as a grown-up was local boy Chris Torment. Suspecting that I had chosen the perfect career, I spent a carefree afternoon watching them do the scene in which the convict, Magwitch, is caught in the marshes, with the younger Pip looking on. Torment wasn't involved. There were a dozen people all fretting over something and no one managing to say or do anything without running a hand through their hair and frowning to their left. But what caught my attention were the three Cadillacs. American military cars, Jeeps and the like, were common in the area because of the air base. But Cadillacs? And men in black suits leaning against them? It was a good peg for my story.

I walked breezily across, reaching for my Marlboros. A man leaning against the side of the front car watched my approach. A bit like the cop watching Janet Leigh in 'Psycho' after she had nicked the money. The man had a crew-cut and was wearing shades. I saw the word 'Cadillac' engraved on the wing mirror. With the boldness of youth, I wanted to take these guys on.

"Hi there. What are you up to way over here?" I offered the man a cigarette. "No one invited you to the party?"

The man looked at me for several seconds without a glimmer of acknowledgement, ignoring the offered cigarette.

"Excuse me?" he said eventually.

I shuffled my feet. "I was just wondering who invited you here. Wondering what you were up to. It's unusual to see American cars in this part of the world and suddenly there are three of them." I looked along the line. The two other drivers, both wearing shades, were also scowling at me. "I mean, three American cars!"

The man in front of me reached into his pocket and pulled out a stick of gum. He was looking beyond me at the film set.

"If I were you, I'd go back the way you came," he said. "You have no business here."

I was squinting into the sun behind the man's face when there wasn't any sun behind him to squint into. Who did this guy think he was? Clint Eastwood?

"Sure. Sorry to have bothered you."

I ambled back to my car, grinning and shaking my head at how I could be so cool. Until I realized that I hadn't been cool. I turned and made the hundred yards back to the Cadillac, still shaking my head and grinning, and this time looking at the ground. I hadn't got my story.

"I'm sorry. But I have to persist. It's my job. Please tell me what you are doing here."

The man looked at me for a while and chewed. He looked bored.

"Beat it," he said.

I kept grinning, watching the man chewing, wondering where I could buy clothes like his and apply for his job.

"One more thing," I said. The man didn't react. "I was just wondering – do you know the way to San Jose?"

The man took some seconds again. "Son, I didn't catch you?"

"Do you know the way to San Jose?" The 'son' bit rankled. "I was wondering if you could tell me."

"San Jose. That's funny. I don't know."

"That's okay. Don't apologise."

"I didn't. Now, please go away." He looked to his left. "Just beat it."

A couple of nights after the 'Great Expectations' shoot, I was driving through patchy, rubbish-strewn woods, singing along to 'Cruel to be Kind', when a car came bouncing up behind me, its lights dazzling me in the mirror. There was more than one car. A line of lights was flickering through the trees. I pulled my Renault 4 off the road and switched off the engine. Three limos flashed by. You could barely hear the engines, just the flashing 'whoosh' noises. I clapped my hands. I followed as fast as I could and was just in time to see the cars turn up a dirt road which I knew led to a silk farm. I followed the single track through trees and rhododendron bushes until I turned a bend and there, on my right, through the hedge, were the lights of the cars.

I stopped my car next to a cricket pavilion and walked on to a mown lawn in front of a magnificent house I had never seen before. It wasn't lit up, but I could see that it was porticoed and pink. A swimming pool with a small diving board was empty and abandoned. A helicopter took up the opposite corner of the lawn, ready for a quick getaway. Leading down from the lawn into some walled garden were marble steps, but they didn't meet up with the lawn. They had slipped back about a yard, like steps meeting – or not meeting – a plane. A drive swept round the side of the grass and along the front of the house. On the drive, in a row, were the three Cadillacs.

I turned and looked back at the cricket pavilion. It seemed out of place – oriental in design, with a curve to the roof. Never had the idea of following up a story appealed to me more, or in such colourful fashion. If I had only one mission, it was to find out what was going on in this place. Cadillacs! A helicopter! A mysterious cricket pavilion!

I got back into my car and drove up the drive. "Come out, come out, wherever you are... Oh shit."

The men were waiting for me in a line across the drive, arms across their chests. One pointed at a space for me to park. I fumbled with the controls and turned on the windscreen wipers instead of turning off the engine. Another opened the car door and asked me to step out. Which I did, saying sorry again and again.

They walked me round the cricket pavilion and in a side door of the house. It was opened by a fat man in white shorts and a tee-shirt, holding a can of beer in his hand. I was thinking about the chances of being kidnapped and held to ransom. I thought about my mum and dad, watching television in a tacky, Victorian-style conservatory just two miles away, wedged on to a modest 1950s house with a leaking roof and damp cellar. I thought briefly about another pretty girl on the rival paper who had a pet sheep.

"Interesting pavilion," I said.

I was escorted into what looked like a kitchen, except that there were no appliances. There was a picture of Sean Connery, Pussy Galore at his side, on the wall above a pool table. There were also a lot of men in the room, sitting on chairs against the walls and talking among themselves. They all wore suits and a couple had pool cues in their hands. One was wearing a shoulder holster. I gulped.

"Guys," the big man said. "I'd like you say hello to…"

"Hadley Arnold."

"He's with the press."

"How did you know that?"

"It's written on your windshield. It says 'press'."

A few raised their arms in greeting and murmured words of welcome. A man with a paunch and dark hair tied back in a ponytail walked over. He was struggling to tuck in his shirt. He put out his hand.

"I'm Joe," he said. "Don't be a berk."

"I'm sorry?"

"I'm playing with you. I said don't be a berk. As an English joke. Because you like your ribald jokes, right? Cockney rhyming slang. Berkshire hunt. What rhymes with hunt? Don't be a berk. What's your name again?"

"Hadley Arnold."

We shook hands. Joe, humming now, appeared to be examining my teeth.

"Hadley Arnold?"

"That's right."

"Are you sure that's not Arnold Hadley?"

"No."

"You're not sure?"

"No. I mean I'm sure."

"Because Arnold is usually a first name."

"No, but really, I'm sure. I know my own name. What order the words are in."

"Good." Joe slapped my arm. "You've come to watch the movie with us?"

"No. I..."

"It's 'On Her Majesty's Secret Service'. Highly under-rated. You want to watch?"

"No, I can't." Tell them why, Hadley. "My father has a hernia."

"Well I'm sorry to hear that. So how can we help you, Harvey?"

"Hadley."

"Hadley. I'm sorry."

"Well, I'm a reporter."

"Okay. Which paper?"

"The Sotobech Sentinel."

"The son-of-a-bitch what?"

"He was at the shoot on the weekend," one of the men said.

I smiled and gave a futile wave. "That's right. I saw you there. I'm sorry if I am intruding. I just wanted to know if you were film producers or something."

"Film producers." Joe looked up. He turned and looked along the line of chairs. "He thinks we're film producers." They chuckled. "Big shot movie producers." He turned back to me. "No, sir, we're not film producers. You're welcome to stay and watch the movie, but there's no story."

"Okay, I'm sorry. I guess I ought to be going."

"We're movie fans, but we're not movie producers." Joe dipped his head. "Tell me, are you a good reporter?"

"I like to think I am, yes. I hope I will be."

"And they train you well up there? At the so-to-bed Sentinel? Shorthand, legal dangers, that kind of thing? The relevant torts?"

"I've only just begun and I'm not sure what a tort is, but yes, they…"

"Integrity, too, I would presume."

"Sorry?"

"They teach you about integrity? I like that in a person. But I'm not sure it can be taught. Not right off the bat."

I shuffled my feet and put my hands in my back pockets. "I don't think I really follow your drift," I said.

"I guess not. Not right off the bat."

"Right. Sorry to have bothered you," I said, eager to be home. I stood for a second and then turned and took giant leaps to the door. Which didn't open. I pulled and pulled until Joe came up behind me and reached for the handle.

"Here, let me get that for you. You have to pull and then turn. It's a little bit awkward." I skipped past him on to the gravel and ran for my car, saying "sorry" a lot as I did so.

"Good luck with your career," Joe shouted. "Keep your head down."

The peg for my 'Great Expectations' story suddenly lost its appeal, except that I had already told the Sotobech Sentinel news editor, from a long line of beet farmers, about the Americans and he thought it was terrific.

"But I don't feel I have enough material."

"Don't be ridiculous. This is unusual and mysterious. We can play with it. I want lots of puns. It will be terrific."

I queued up my typewriter, waited until the news editor had gone, wondered why he had spat the word "puns" in my face, and sank my head into my arms. Then came a flash, or rather lower-than-simmer, puttering, blue-flamed back-burner gas, of inspiration.

"The people of Sotobech have their own Great Expectations for a best-of-British movie production of the classic made here in the Fens, but they can be forgiven for asking what the Dickens all those Americans were doing on the set."

The story was published at just two hundred words with lots

of pictures of the actors and none showing the American cars. It was a truly awful read and the page was poorly designed with no one big picture to set it all off. The headline was a ball-grabbing 'Great Expectations in the Fens' and at the grand old age of twenty-one, I knew the only headline to pull in any reader to such a piece of fluff would be something like 'Let's get laid in the Fens'. It was unfit to join my then still thin file of cuttings and I was happy to consign the movie, and the Americans, and the story, to history.

At least, I was happy about it at the time.

My cell phone brought me back to the present. It was Baxter up on the twenty-third floor.

"We need that fucking intestines story. It's still on your screen."

"Yup. I'm just coming up."

"The hills are alive with intestines. Don't let it get too technical."

"Okay."

"We don't want it to be too medical."

"Okay."

CHAPTER FOUR

Shrubs was an old-fashioned news agency, in that it still peddled news. Some of the bigger agencies had turned their attention to the financial markets, and a story was only a story if it had implications for investors. In layman terms, it meant every story was long, analytical and hugely important, leaving little room for the man-bites-dog stories which were Shrubs's bread and butter.

For the most part, its correspondents were inexperienced and rough round the edges. That's where the Hong Kong desk was supposed to kick in – we had senior journalists, mostly British, American, Indian or Australian, who could clean up the copy quickly and move it out. But some of the deskers were pretty awful. They had carved reasonably successful careers while being awful, knowing next to nothing about grammar, spelling or the law. Or how to write. Or how to edit. I was often in awe of their ignorance, and of my own, and of Baxter's style of news editing. A cruiser sank off the U.S. West Coast during the Hong Kong desk's control period, i.e. when everyone in California was either fast asleep or out rollerblading down some boardwalk wearing nothing but a thong, and I was taking the story off CNN. Baxter exploded from his office. He too had been watching CNN, which was now showing a coastguard helicopter flying low over debris lying thick in the water. He leant over my shoulder and pointed at the screen. I breathed in his cheap, chirpy after-shave which had a name like 'Turbo' or 'Exhaust Bay'.

"Is that helicopter pink?" Baxter asked.

I was not immediately sure of the significance but in any case, it was difficult to tell. It was dusk on the West Coast and the colour of the helicopter was just too close to call.

"I'm not sure," I said.

"No, it's pink. Look at it."

"It could be pink. Or it could be the light. You want me to write that it was a pink helicopter searching for survivors? As opposed to a blue one, or a green one? Do you think it's worth the risk?"

"It's a pink helicopter. What do you say, Hadley?"

Give me a gun. "It does look pink *now*, but we wouldn't want to get it wrong. I can't see any insignia, but isn't it unlikely the coastguard would fly around in pink helicopters?"

"Of course it's pink. You want to know why?" I didn't. "It's a gay helicopter. From San Francisco, most likely. Pinkie, pinkie helicopter. From San Francisco." A cackling Baxter returned triumphantly to his office, slamming the door behind him.

The New Delhi bureau had written, on a Monday, a curtain-raiser to the Pope's visit, beginning: '*The Pope arrives in the Indian capital on Friday hoping to erase years of distrust*' etc, etc. The story was allotted to the English sub, Rupert, he of the violently shaking legs, whose life-long editorial mission was to hunt down the word 'witness' and change it to 'eye-witness' (as opposed to ear, nose or throat witness) and who wanted to make an 'urgent' (a couple of paragraphs moved super fast) out of it.

"Why?" I asked.

"Because he's arrived four days earlier than scheduled. He's already there."

"What are you talking about?"

"It says he arrives."

"It says he arrives on Friday."

"How can he arrive on Friday?"

"What?"

"It says he 'arrives'. Between you and me, that's the present tense. Is, was and always will be."

"I cannot believe this. The copy says he arrives on Friday. If he'd already arrived, it would have said he arrived on Monday."

"How can he arrive on Friday? Friday is in the future."

"So you want to say the Pope will arrive on Friday?"

"Not if he has already arrived today."

I was thinking of either stabbing Rupert with my pen or launching a dramatic change in career when Baxter again exploded from his office.

"I heard the last bit of this and there is no doubt in my mind that the Pope is still due to arrive on Friday. A simple phone call would solve it once and for all."

I was calmed and grateful. "Thank you, Rodney."

"The only possible area of confusion is whether he means this Friday or next."

"What?"

"The pontiff."

"You're right," Rupert chimed in. "There's another question for you. It's pluperfect."

"Another question for me? What do you mean it's pluperfect?"

My self-proclaimed area of expertise was spelling. The computer system once had a built-in spellchecker, but it was useless in spotting the wrong use of 'effect' or 'affect', 'it's' or 'its'... It was useless anyway. It would throw up suggestions that were unscientific and ridiculous and which occasionally got on to the wire. Hadley Arnold, only once though, came out as Hardly Armchair. When it replaced former Chinese President Jiang Zemin with Jingo Semen, the whole thing was disabled. So was the sub who let it through after Baxter ran him down in his Hyundai Sonata. My reputation as a speller was reinforced, I thought, by a test of ten everyday words I would give to people and which I would preface by saying that I had learnt it from my uncle when I was kid and he had said the average score, among educated

Englishmen, was two.

I would also make clear that what was an everyday word in the first half of the twentieth century was not necessarily so at the beginning of the twenty-first. I would also make it clear that my uncle, long since dead, had spent most of his adult life in colonial Africa where expats had had time on their hands and drunk a lot of gin on verandas.

One quiet afternoon, I gave the test to Baxter, who put his feet up on his desk confidently, leant back and stared at the ceiling.

"Hit me," he said.

A great idea. The words were: embarrass (tricky – two 'r's or one?), harass (same!), rarefy (you're kidding, an 'e'?) vilify (cool!), supersede (whoa!), desiccate (no, no, you're wrong), pla-guy (what the fuck is that?), picnicking (silence), inoculate (you have to be kidding) and innuendo (um).

Baxter scored zero. Nil points. He dismissed me from his of-fice and a week later fired off a letter of reprimand which was to go on my file, although what future generations of news editors would make of it was unclear.

"You may think you have embarrassed, or even harassed, me with your ludicrous spelling test which appears to be 'out of Africa'. But it has since been superseded by events, so don't think you can use it to vilify me. Your desiccated test is anyway inaccurate since I have since found that plaguy is extinct. Not that I am one to hold a grugue (sic), so I won't ask you, willy-nilly, to name the last five secretary-generals of the United Nations."

It was a constant battle of asserting one's authority in a field in which all the stars were out reporting in any number of tongues and writing seamless copy, not sitting at desks and look-ing glum. And looking more and more glum the older they got; age could be cruel to wire service subs. Experience, in the most part but with notable exceptions, didn't seem to add value. It just made someone who had managed to get 'commitment' right for twenty years start spelling it with a 'k'. I had read a piece about the Sultan of Johor playing golf in Malaysia. It said that when he hit a bad shot, he would turn, grimacing, and scan the horizon to make sure no one had seen it and be angry if they had. The writer described it as a '360-degree scowl'. For subs on the Hong Kong desk, their entire working life was a 360-degree scowl. For the few who had a grasp of history (count me out here), there was some point to them being there. Most of those who claimed a grasp of grammar or the law didn't know the difference between a transitive verb and Perry Mason.

"You can't say 'if it were'."

"It's the subjunctive."

"Oh please."

"But it is."

"We aren't supposed to use split infinitives."

"It's not a split infinitive!"

"Especially in the pluperfect."

Very few of the subs knew anything useful about the law. Someone would get charged with murder in Australia and the police would say he had confessed and Shrubs would run the story, breaking every rule (breaking every tort!) in the book. The law of contempt – under British law, which is what Shrubs used – says as soon as someone has been charged with a crime, you shut up. You can give details of what happened, like someone was shot and died three hours later, but you can't start pinning the blame on anyone as the case is now *sub judice*, which is Latin for 'steer the fuck clear of this'. You certainly can't say anyone has confessed, unless they did the confessing in court by pleading guilty, and you certainly can't start accusing people of doing things when they haven't been charged. I was explaining some of these points to a bearded Englishman called Tim who was frothing at the mouth over a story that quoted police in Thailand as saying they knew the man in their custody, who had been charged and named, was the man they wanted in the case of the flashing of a high-ranking politician because he had a 'singular willy', just as the politician had said.

"This is a great, great story," Tim said. "He had a singular willy!"

"But we can't touch it," I said.

"Can't touch his willy," said Tim. "Ha, ha! We can't touch his willy!"

Baxter came out of his office with a smile growing on his face and I put my head in my hands.

"We can't touch his willy," Baxter said. "Willy, willy, willy!"

A lot of stress in my working day came from the effort of hiding my own select empty pools of knowledge and covering up for the lapses in concentration. Budget days scared me. Not because I was afraid of the vast amount of copy, the speed at which it would arrive and the speed at which it was meant to go out, but because none of it made any sense. It was all bollocks. There was no point of focus. In ordinary news – real news about crashes and diseases and people caught bonking in business class on planes – there were guidelines. Five dead in a pile-up caused by a cow wandering across a road in New Delhi isn't a story because it happens all the time. Five dead in a pileup caused by a cow wandering across Piccadilly is a great story. Twenty killed when a train runs into a truck carrying a wedding party in rural Pakistan is three paragraphs. Twenty killed, including one American, when the same train runs into the truck is ten paragraphs, to be updated as soon as the United States woke up. But in economic news, there did not seem to be any threshold; all any crack head had to do was stand up and say something about a currency or a long bond and Shrubs would run the story. A bulletin, then the urgent, then the full story, running up to a hundred lines or more. It was all about feeding fat, rich people information to make them fatter and richer. That was it! Romance and adventure and colour scored nil points. And when the nonsense budget copy came overflowing with numbers, numbers that represented 'economic indicators', it was time to consider pooing in the pants and looking for the nearest exit.

CHRIS TORMENT slipped into Hong Kong quietly, but not quietly enough for me not to notice. There it was, on the back page of the South China Morning Post, which had allocated three paragraphs to the event: "Torment Arrives". The sub responsible for that gem of a headline didn't know the half of it.

It wasn't long before I saw my old nemesis. I was in Tsim Sha Tsui, the tourist shopping bit of the Kowloon peninsula, where I had picked up some sheet music for my sister's birthday, specifically 'Cantonese Opera from the Southern Song Dynasty', which was a crowd favourite. Pamela, a good bit younger than me, was tone deaf.

I walked slap bang into a film crew on Nathan Road outside the sleazy Chungking Mansions, which was a fire-trap warren of Indian restaurants, backpacker hostels, unkempt flats with gold smugglers on short leases, travel agencies and shady money dealerships. Torment looked like an American vice-president. Expensively groomed. It seemed that among the dozens involved in making this film, all huddled together on the pavement with clipboards, cups and earphones, no one could do anything without running it by him – without having a laugh, a turn. They bantered with Torment while the rest of the world – pedestrians packed at this time of day like wildebeest on the run and forced to step into the busiest road in Kowloon just to get by – looked across, tripped, looked again and wondered who these people were.

Sipping a McDonald's coffee, I monitored every self-conscious turn of Torment's head, the pushing back of the hair, the wide smiles – gestures I remembered from decades earlier and hated anew.

Some action. Torment reached up with a light meter or hygrometer or some other cinematic device, and targeted it at the roof of the Holiday Inn. All heads were turned his way. He read the dial. I heard him gush: "This looks really good."

I chose my quiet words carefully: "What a fuckwit."

Torment was handsome, no doubt, and in good trim. But there was something missing. Some substance. Some part of the age-ing process seemed to have passed him by, despite the graying hair. He gave the impression of being the same age he had been at school. Like a big, bullying, white paper bag, heavy makeup hiding the cruelty lines. What was he doing, always cavorting? The truth now: he liked to be liked. Torment had spent his entire adult life prancing, trying to make people like him. He had al-lowed himself no time to consolidate.

I saw Candy Kam. And there was Panda Koo, wearing fur and smoking what looked, from where I was standing, like a pipe. There was fur all round her head, as if these were the play-ing fields of Halfords, not Hong Kong. I looked at her face and lips and thought of her without a stitch of clothing on. She would be chilly, first off, and something would have to be done about that. I wondered if, at that very moment, there could be anyone as attractive, anywhere. The director, Adolf Lee, was standing on the roof of a bus and I wondered, after I'd finished thinking about Panda Koo stark naked, if he had done a bit of casting couch hanky-panky. Maybe casting couch hanky-panky was all Adolf Lee ever did in between shoots like this when he would celebrate by climbing on to the roof of a bus. I walked closer, caught Candy's eye and pushed my way through.

Candy gave me a quick, half smile and then looked down at her clipboard.

"What are they waiting for?" I asked. Candy mumbled some-thing I couldn't catch. "For a minute there, I had a bit of a wry chuckle. I thought maybe you were all waiting for me to clear off. You know, wait until the amateurs were out of the way."

Candy didn't look up. I was focused on the back of her head and smiling.

"They are waiting for the new light meter," she said.

"I'm sorry?"

"The important light meter. They are waiting for it."

"I see."

This was the woman who would get me into the movies. She *was* getting me into the movies, according to Joe, albeit with Torment. A one in a million chance. The fame thing was bollocks, I was sure. The closest thing to it I had known was an occasional by-line in the Jakarta Post, the Bangkok Post, or the South China Morning Post. Or walking out of an airport with hundreds of eyes on you, at your weathered face and baggage. And then you are among all those people who had their eyes on you, and they now had their eyes on someone else. You were just a departure, or an arrival, or another nob with a trolley. Torment had never been the nob with the trolley, that was the point. Even back at our crappy school, Torment had a thing for the movies. He also had a thing for high-brow opera, the theatre and pre-war German electrical appliances. He wore cravats at weekends and gave impromptu poetry readings in the bog. When he wasn't bullying or beating, conspiring or caning, he ponced around the place like a right Oscar Wilde. Even on a good day, Torment would make my life a misery.

Athletic, good looking and academically dull, Torment had played the lead in all the school plays. I hadn't, but I had been in a lot of school plays. I was a pirate in 'The Pirates of Penzance'. I'd played a boy in 'Oliver!'. My most challenging role, as mentioned, was as Queen Anne in 'Richard III', wearing the billowing gown and white pointy hat. And Torment had played Richard! That play had gone to Holland in the Easter holidays. I had smoked cigarettes in the wings.

"Put that cigarette down, before I Gravel you and send you to Big Track," Torment had barked. "What's the matter with you?"

What was the matter with me? What was the matter with him? What was he talking about?

Within three or four years, the now puffed-up Chris Torment

was a name in English television, appearing in Jane Austen and George Eliot serialisations. At twenty-two, he played the vicar, Mr Elton, in a big-screen version of 'Emma'. I went to see it at a huge, cold cinema in Wisbech. Alone in the circle, I watched Elton mince around Emma like some tacky Disney-on-Ice manoeuvre until she tells him where to get off.

"You tell him, Emma. The moron."

Next came a couple more TV series, some World War Two prisoner-of-war nonsense. Halfords, abandoned for the Christmas holidays, doubled as a German castle. This was the BBC's idea of Colditz. Everyone thought the wind noises were great at first, but they went on and on. A bit over the top. Actors were getting ear infections and the wind had to be edited out. Then a couple more movies until it was time for the English press to speculate on Chris Torment taking over as the next James Bond, for heaven's sake. He never did, or hadn't yet – surely he couldn't ever? Torment was now in his forties, I reminded myself again cheerfully. Middle-aged.

Torment and Joe. What were they up to? Who *were* these guys?

Earlier in my career, I had laid out feature pages for a London Sunday tabloid. One edition was devoted to speculation about who should take over as the next James Bond, as the incumbent at the time, Roger Moore, was getting on a bit. The pictures and words I had been given were all about young wet English actors, who were all Chris Torment in one way or another. Patrick Mower of 'Callan', 'Target' and more recently 'Emmerdale' fame, got a mention and was looking good, I remembered. There were also a couple of loose-jawed Americans. Neither Timothy Dalton nor Pierce Brosnan got a look in. Mower certainly was not the favourite for the 'licence to kill mantle', according to the festering pile of words I had to deal with, which used the phrase 'licence to kill mantle' five times. A poll of the readers, James Bond aficionados every one, had put Richard Gere at the top of the list. One reader was quoted as saying he had chosen Gere "because he didn't look like a right prat". But if some prat had to play James Bond, it had to be a British prat, and Patrick McGoohan (long my choice for the role) was by then far too old.

This was the gist of the words that slopped onto the page under a few pictures of the leading candidates (inset of Patrick McGoohan). Thunderballs.

TWO WEEKS after the audition, I was summoned back to the Lion Dance Practice Room for an evening promotion party for the film. The cast of thousands was to be there, and I was one of them. I was to meet Adolf Lee and co-producer Gretel, Panda Koo and Torment. A letter from Gretel's assistant said my "unbounded enthusiasm" during the audition had won them all over and would I be free for forty-eight hours to rehearse and shoot my part, which would include some lines.

I was in the door of the entertainment business. I had made it. I told the others on the Shrubs desk and cheers went up. The gaunt Fagin, whose desktop popcorn machine had been stolen, walked across and clapped me on the back.

"You arsehole," he said and walked away.

A tall, young American came over. "I heard that. What's with him?"

"No, it was friendly. A term of endearment. He was congratulating me. He's Scottish."

I was given a script with the cast list (preliminary) stapled to the front. Someone had moved pretty fast. I searched for my name. It was like being back at school. There was Chris Torment at the top. Very near the bottom was the entry:

GLUM MAN IN BAR — HADLEY ARNOLD

Glum. That's okay. I could do glum. I skipped through the pages but couldn't pin down my lines. I started reading at random. Page seventeen...

>   MRS HOLLAND
> As you know the West Country is famed for
> many things: moors, beaches, cream. Many
> famous writers have found their inspira-
> tion there. Many people who, in the inno-
> cence of youth, have seen their lives in
> distant fields, have returned to the West
> Country because that is where, first and
> last, they be drawn.

>   NORMAN
> Good heavens.

> COLONEL (in thick Devonshire accent)
> Please go on. That's where they be drawn.

>   MRS HOLLAND
> So imagine my dilemma as a Somerset pot-
> ter...

I found myself retching, like I did when I smoked without a drink. I dipped in again, at page seventy-three. Scott was speaking. Torment was Scott.

>   SCOTT
> Someone once said Brighton, a resort on the
> south coast of England, always looks like
> it's been helping police with their inqui-
> ries. Well, Hong Kong is like that too. She
> has her own persona.

>   LING-LING

What's that?

SCOTT
She's a grand, confused duchess in a string
of pearls. She's bedecked with gems that
dangle and twinkle from the dank hilltops
of Victoria..."

I felt a stab of pain behind my right eye and hoped I wasn't coming down with something. I hoped I hadn't been bedecked by a bug. And who was Victoria? I imagined Ling-ling saying "What's that?". Like in the 'Teletubbies'. You fool, Scott. She isn't asking about Hong Kong's persona. She's asking what a persona is! I persevered, skipped a few pages, glanced askance at page forty-four...

MAGNUS
So Philip, how's that young filly of yours?

PHILIP
Not too shabby actually.

MAGNUS
That's good, because I was wondering...

It was touch and go, but I managed to keep my bowels closed. But hold on, this was the bar in the FCC. I was the 'glum man in bar'. I flicked through the pages. Nothing. Nothing. And then:

SCOTT
There's something they're not telling us,
Magnus. I've been racking my brains...

MAGNUS

It's the new regime, Scott.

GLUM MAN IN BAR
Here, where have all the babes gone? You
want a crisp?

I searched for my next line, but it seemed that was it. I read it again and scrutinised it for hidden meaning, innuendo. Apparently it was some kind of comic relief, the drunk club bore, glum, breaking up a serious conversation with a question about babes. Hmm, I could do something with that. Perhaps a lurch away from camera as I look for the girls – maybe I see one just before I say 'babes'. It would require a sharp double-take, a lascivious, drawn-out "helloooo", like Leslie Phillips in one of the 'Doctor in the House' films. It would be a challenge. I could spill my drink. Perhaps I could put on a stutter. That was it – the upper-class twit reporter soaking up the booze in the former colony. *D-, d-,d-, do you want a cr-, cr-, crisp?* Plenty of material there to discuss with Adolf and his aides. But there was the rub, I thought, feeling the collywobbles coming on again, setting off through the colon and hovering in the chest. I had yet to meet Torment and I didn't want to meet Torment. Would I be able to disguise my sneering contempt?

I crossed the floor of the Lion Dance Practice Room thinking: am I disguising my sneering contempt? Chris Torment was holding court, expanding, jabbing, lecturing and expostulating. I felt like I was approaching a crowd gathered around a street magician. I was welcomed by two pretty assistants, met a couple of fellow extras and had a word with Gretel. I listened to a welcoming speech by Adolf Lee in which the stars were introduced to the crowd as Torment looked down and shuffled his feet, trying to seem bashful. I saw the hint of a smirk. Who did Torment think he was fooling? But he got a lot of applause, as did the immaculate Panda Koo, who looked as arrogant as Torment was trying to look shy. She wore loose khaki jeans, a white top show-ing a bare midriff, and had her hair tied back in a ponytail. Suzie Wong eating melon seeds on the Star Ferry.

Torment was now barking a series of pompous lies, shimmy-ing and gesticulating all over the shop. I forced my malevolent scowl into a smile, swallowed hard, lowered my head and lis-tened.

"... but of course this is not my first time in the tropics, if indeed we are indeed in the tropics..." (Some of the audience, mostly Chinese girls, laughed at this. They *laughed*.) "... actually I'm not sure where we are. Is it, is it a bird, a plane?"

The laughs, again. I thought: what kind of world is this?

"But seriously," he went on, "of course, what one loves most about the tropics, at least from my point of view, is that ability, that sheer wanton..." Torment was searching for the *mot juste*, staring at the ceiling, drumming his free hand at the air, the fin-gers of the other hand dipped into a tight, gold-braided waist-coat pocket. "That sheer wanton call of nature, if you will, to sleep *au naturel*, with the windows wide open."

No one, I realized, knew what Torment was on about. He was just a big, loud, famous gweilo with flailing arms and a weak face. There was some polite tittering behind hands as a couple of the girls caught on that he was saying something slightly ris-qué. I was thinking: life is too short. Torment had brushed his gaze across me a couple of times during his speech, but there was no sign of recognition. How did I look now compared with back then? A scary thought. The hair was much the same, but I wore glasses now and many of the blood vessels in my nose had exploded within the last few years, blown to smithereens by booze. And the eyes – the eyes definitely had had it. At Halfords, desperate for some sort of street credibility as a rogue, I applied a touch of black Kiwi shoe polish under my eyes. I wanted bags. I walked into the corridor outside my study and the other boys had looked at me, stared at my face, but did not speak. They were thinking: why has this prick put boot polish under his eyes? I thought they were thinking: look at Hadley. He's been doing serious drugs.

Well, now I didn't need shoe polish to achieve the effect. Anyway, the memory ended, of course, with Torment appearing at the end of the corridor, his cane under his arm, looking like a German officer.

"What's the matter with you boy?" he bellowed as I automatically came to attention. Torment approached and sniffed.

"Have you been smoking, you New Track Gym?"

"No, Torment."

"What have you done to your eyes, you little girl? Are you wearing make-up, you jam roll? Answer me before I Hankle you at Big Track and trace Potatoes on Twenty Place."

Hello? Let's stop here. What language are you speaking, please? I am a student of etymology and am drawing blanks from every planet known to man.

That's what I would have liked to have said, but of course didn't.

Back in Hong Kong in the present, someone dared to challenge Torment.

"Mr Torment," a young Chinese executive said. "I must see all your films that we in Hong Kong can see. Surely to sleep with the air-con is to be more comfortable, no?"

He had Torment up against the ropes, no doubt about it. Torment folded his arms on his chest and furrowed his brow. Had to think about this one.

"No, you're wrong there. From my experience. Even allowing for the mosquitoes. I think you're wrong there."

"You like mosquitoes, Mr Torment?"

"I like all forms of life. I've learnt to respect all forms of life. You have to in this business. When a mosquito bites me, I think, yes, this is what you do. I must give you space. Go on, bite me."

I kept a rigid smile on my face as my fingernails bit blood

from the palms of my hands.

"But I'll tell you what, young man," Torment went on. "What's your name?"

"Chen."

"I'll tell you what, Chen." I saw a mischievous smile growing on Torment's face and prepared to wince. "I give mosquitoes space, and will continue to do so, lying in the nude, as long as they don't bite my beef bayonet. And they haven't yet."

Probably haven't been able to find it. I tried to suppress an involuntary, wailing groan that turned into something like laughter. The noise turned a few heads.

"Sorry, what is the reference?" Chen said. "I don't understand."

"Never mind, never mind." Torment turned away to accept a drink from a pretty aide.

"Sorry, what is the reference?" Chen repeated to Torment's back, but Torment ignored him.

I was planning my next move, wondering whether this was the time to re-introduce myself to my previous school buddy. Or maybe to go to Chen and explain what kind of arsehole Torment was. I turned to Chen, who was staring at Torment and trembling. Chen's eyes met mine for a moment and then turned back to Torment, who had his hand around the shoulders of the pretty Chinese girl and was leading her away from the group.

Chen crouched and put his glass on the floor. He pulled an envelope from his inside jacket pocket and slid it across the polished wood towards me.

Then he stood up and pulled a silver pistol out of another pocket. He was sweating and looked mad.

"Sorry, I didn't catch the reference," he said.

Torment was fifteen feet away and mingling. The room went quiet, but for the giggle of a movie babe, the bray of an old bore and the lingering clink of a glass. Chen was pointing the pistol at Torment, and the crowd parted to give him a clear line of vision. Strange that, I thought afterwards – but then again, this was Chris Torment. The guests had retreated about a yard to each side, leaving me the nearest to Chen. This was one of those defining moments. What to do?

I looked at the envelope Chen had slid across the floor and considered my options. I could bend to pick it up and then launch myself at Chen, pinning his gun hand against the wall. Or perhaps I could try diverting his attention – I could make a high-pitched screech, like a monkey, or a low hoot, like an owl (I had learnt how to do that at Halfords, blowing through my thumbs into cupped hands. I could also do a cuckoo) – and then, when the surprised Chen turned, I could launch myself at his legs and hopefully send the gun clattering to the ground.

For the time being though, I watched Chen hold the gun in two hands stretched in front of him.

"No one say a word," Chen said. "Please no one do anything silly. This is between me and him."

I saw Torment gulp and fidget. He was gearing himself up to say something, to play the hero.

"Mr Torment, you will stay quiet, no?" Chen said as Torment put his hands up.

I was now leaning towards a third option. This involved crying. Inconsolable, I would collapse slowly towards the ground, and then hurl my body at Chen, winding him enough to drop the pistol. Decisions, decisions.

"I will make this speedy," Chen said. "Your acting has proved derogatory of minorities and you lack goodness. I represent an organization which has been offended. In reference to your Shakespeare in the Park, last year in the selfsame Regent's Park, I say goodnight sweet prince..."

Chen cocked the hammer. A gasp went up and Torment winced and flailed his arms in front of his face as if shooing off bees. I stirred into action at last. Chen took a deep, quick intake of breath and I bundled into him, just as he pulled the trigger.

The hammer went click.

And that was it

Chen was staring hard at me as I lay on top of him on the floor, his face six inches from mine.

"Damn it," he said, offering no resistance.

In one swift movement, he slid his hand around and fired the gun at his head. This time I winced.

Again nothing happened. I got up.

"It's okay," I said to two security men who were picking Chen off the floor. "No one's hurt."

One of the security men looked at me quizzically, turned to Chen, lifted him up and punched him in the stomach. Chen fell to the floor again and made no more sound. The chatter began as the now limp Chen was carried out of the room.

The crowd filled the space and I brushed myself down. Torment was already jabbering to everyone around him. "Well, there you have it", was one inane comment I heard. Then: "Well done, you over there."

I acknowledged this with a small wave.

"That was an extraordinarily brave thing to do," a pretty Cantonese girl said, briefly putting her hand on my back, before disappearing into the crowd.

Two men in suits wearing earphones approached Torment and suggested he leave with them. One of them kicked the envelope on the floor in my direction without realising.

I picked it up and put it in my pocket.

CHAPTER FIVE

I DON'T LIKE the idea of big news stories before they happen, but relish them when they fall into my lap and the opposition is nowhere in sight. I clapped my hands like a teacher before his class. The blood began to flow and my moves became faster and more instinctive. I called the desk.

"Fagin? It's me."

"What do you want at this hour?"

"This is serious. Torment. Someone tried to assassinate Torment."

"Assassinate Torment? Can you assassinate an actor?"

"Someone tried to kill Torment. I want to give you an urgent."

"Is he wounded?"

"No. The gun didn't go off."

"Where was this?"

"At the party to introduce the cast. Some Chinese guy pulled a gun on Torment and pulled the trigger. But it didn't go off. Then he tried to kill himself, but it didn't go off again."

"It sounds like a lot of things didn't happen. Are you sure it's even a story?"

"Look…" I heard muffled sounds as Fagin consulted whoever else was on the desk at the time. It was around ten o'clock.

"Okay, let's give it a shot," Fagin said.

"British movie actor Chris Torment escaped…"

"What's the source?"

"I'm the source. I was there."

"You sure it was a real gun? What do the police say?"

"This has only just happened. I saw it. It was real. I can get a police comment later. I grabbed the guy. They're waiting right now to talk to me."

"You grabbed him? You saved Torment's life, you bastard?"

"I know. But I didn't save him. I just kind of grabbed the guy and fell on top of him."

"Who was it?"

"I don't know. Some Chinese guy. Wait, wait..." I remembered the envelope. "I've got some stuff. Some statement, wait. I'm just looking at it now. He's from Sri Lanka."

"A Chinese gunman from Sri Lanka? Look, if this is a joke..."

"He's from a group called DALJC."

"Dulch? Never heard of it. It's double Dulch. Seriously, have you been drinking?"

"I'm not making this up. They're initials. DALJC. Democratic Association for the Liberation of Jaffna Chinese. He's pissed off with Torment's movies. His group wants a separate homeland on some island called Macho, north of Sri Lanka."

"Chinese in Sri Lanka? They want a homeland?"

"That's what it says."

"What on earth for? I've never heard of Macho. Macho ado about nothing, I reckon. Give us what you've got. Wait. What do they say about Torment?"

"His movies are derogatory of minorities. Lack integrity."

"His movies are shit. Go on."

"Okay. British movie star Chris Torment escaped an assassination attempt by a Sri Lankan Chinese gunman..."

"What? You want to make people laugh? Give me the shooting bit. A lone gunman opened fire on British movie star Chris Torment..."

"How can we say opened fire when the gun didn't go off?"

"A lone gunman pulled a pistol..."

"It was more than that. He pulled the trigger."

"Well, we can't say it was an assassination attempt."

"Okay. How about escaped with his life?"

"Escaped unharmed."

"Okay. British movie actor Chris Torment escaped unharmed when his would-be killer..."

"Would-be killer?"

"He pulled the trigger."

"Maybe it was just a publicity stunt. Maybe he never meant the gun to go off. And maybe it wasn't real. Anyway it's ugly. And we have someone in custody, I presume, and no charges. Has anyone been charged?"

"Um."

"British film star Chris Torment escaped unharmed when an apparent pistol..."

"An apparent pistol?"

"A pistol-like object."

"*A pistol-like object?*"

"British movie star Chris Torment escaped what appeared to be a botched assassination attempt at a Hong Kong party to launch his new film."

I thought for a while. "How can you escape a botched assassination attempt? If it was botched, there's nothing to escape."

"Piss off. It's good. Give me one more paragraph."

I sighed. "A lone gunman, claiming to represent a Sri Lankan separatist group for, er, Chinese, fired at Torment but the gun failed to go off, a witness said. I'll call back with the rest."

"That is awful. And shouldn't we get in here that he's tipped to be the next James Bond?"

"Oh, please."

"What? Oh please let's get it in here? Or oh please let's not?"

"He's not going to be the next James Bond."

"How old is he?"

"I don't know. Sixty?"

"Don't be ridiculous."

TWO DAYS LATER, Torment visited Shrubs to soak up the atmosphere. The Asia-Pacific desk was abuzz. Chinese secretaries and copy girls were whispering and giggling, hands held in front of their mouths, tripping from one group to another, from the pantry to the front desk to the water cooler, ignoring the backpacker in the lift lobby selling wholemeal sandwiches. There were also about a dozen expatriate children on a school outing wandering about, learning first hand that the last job they would ever want in life was that of a desker with Shrubs. I watched them all with a grimace. What was all the commotion about? Ever since the assassination attempt story, Torment had become even more of a celebrity. And he hadn't done anything! It was all so unfair. Celebrity feeds on nothing and just grows and grows.

"What's all the fuss about?" the backpacker asked me.

"Bloody good question."

The Asia-Pacific deskers had their heads down as if it were business as usual – Baxter had stressed that that was to be the case. A note had been posted on the board saying that Torment would survey the journalists at work and would likely ask some questions. It was also possible that he would sit at an empty desk, uninvited, or suddenly speak urgently into a phone, slam a drawer, or berate an imagined colleague. The deskers were not to be alarmed, were not to interrupt and were to 'take into consideration' the recent attempt on his life. I let out an involuntary bray at this. But the real kicker was the last paragraph.

"Should any staff be addressed by Mr Torment, please be advised that under no circumstances should he or she look him in the eye. Mr Torment is very sensitive to unscheduled attention."

Say what? Unscheduled attention? The man's in the movies and he's sensitive to attention? He would burst into tears if people *didn't* look him in the eye.

The morning passed. The schoolchildren dispersed around the office, interviewing various deskers. Just keep clear of Rupert. And me, for that matter. I had subbed up a couple of cricket stories and the day's Hong Kong political story into which I had tried to insert the phrase "unscheduled attention" from various vantage points, but none seemed to work. I was rolling up imaginary shirtsleeves, preparing myself for butchering a feature on Asian Gay Week, Torment all but forgotten, when the door burst open and in swept a veritable motorcade of people, checking the ceiling, speaking into phones, walking fast, black flex in hand, ignoring everybody, round the corner, through photographic, past television. There were ten of them at the very least. I heard a walkie-talkie voice say something about the "party" being expected in seconds. The door shut behind them.

The Asia-Pacific desk was agape. Rupert's legs started shaking. Notices were still fluttering on the board in the slipstream; the note about Torment had fallen to the floor.

There was a knock on the door. All eyes turned. Nothing happened.

"Please don't look at me."

This was Candy, who had swept in with the rest. She was now at the far end of the room and looking very nervous. She meant don't look at *him*. The idiot outside. Someone was trying the door, but it had an automatic security lock. Candy ran forward, all twenty-five yards, and opened it. I admired her bottom. The subs turned away and sat rigid. Candy was speaking to someone, presumably Torment, evidently telling him not to be such a prat.

"No don't be," I heard her say. "There are nice, handsome people here."

Never mind. In he came, walking erect, head held high like John Gielgud. He was wearing a safari jacket – a safari *suit* no less, and I was prepared to bet money he was completely pissed.

The office was silent for a moment until a phone stirred everyone back to life. They were stirred again when Torment bellowed:

"Get that phone! This could be the big one!"

I had been in the news business a long time, but had never heard a line beginning to resemble that. All the instincts were misplaced. A young cadet frowned, hesitated, whispered "shit" and picked up the phone.

"Thank you," he said and listened a bit. "Yes, thank you. I understand." He hung up. "It's the sandwich man," he told everyone solemnly, avoiding Torment's glare. "He's in the lobby. Only cheese and pickle left and he's leaving in five minutes."

The keyboards started up like cicadas. Torment appeared to stumble, and the keyboards stopped again. Everyone was looking, but not looking, at the tall, familiar dickhead who went into a crouch and, breathing heavily, pulled out a gun.

"Oh lord," I whispered.

"No one look at me."

Torment swung the gun round the desk and the assembled journos, one by one, remembered to avert their gaze. They all knew instinctively to duck. The children were staring at Torment, their mouths open.

"That man's got a gun," one of them said. Brilliant.

Torment loped along the aisle and then slammed his back against the wall. He looked terrified. He looked barmy. Torment caught my eye.

"Don't look now, Senator," he cried. "Not until the crow makes wing to the rooky wood. If you get my drift."

I recognized something Shakespearean but didn't know what the fuck he was on about. I looked at Candy who in turn looked earnest, focused. This was normal, it seemed. Dear, oh dear. Torment was fumbling in his pockets now.

"Take the gun," he said to no one in particular. Then he threw it on the floor. "I never want to see it again."

He turned to Baxter, who was also looking and not looking at the same time, arms folded over his gut and under his gullet.

"And I never want to see your ugly face again either," Torment said.

Things were picking up. Baxter turned to his colleagues with a 'what did I do' look on his face. A phone rang and everyone stopped. The Canadian sub answered.

"I'm not at my desk," he said after a while with some urgency. "I'm going to my desk now." Then away from the receiver: "It's a bomb in Peshawar."

He pulled the phone over to his desk leaving the cord stretched taut about a foot high across the floor. It was obvious what was going to happen. He logged on super-fast to his terminal and said:

"Shoot."

Which was exactly what the phone did, from between the Canadian sub's shoulder and his ear, as Torment bounded in the direction of Baxter and tripped on the cord.

The Canadian was left in shock, his head bent over with his ear to his shoulder and nothing to listen to in between. Torment, oblivious to real, hard news, was about to make some more of his own brand.

With a muffled "why you bastard", he leapt over one of the desks, landed a yard in front of Baxter and slugged him.

There was silence again. One person clapped.

"Never..." Torment said, looking down at my boss who was crawling away fast, saying, "he hit me, he hit me" under his breath, "...never tell me I'm off a story."

Torment was walking backwards around the desk the way he had come. He was gasping.

"This story is mine," he said. "My lifeline!"

And then whispering, his voice shaking: "My life!"

Torment was at the entrance now, panting and fumbling for the handle behind him. Making gargling noises and pointing to the ceiling, he slipped out and closed the door. Cries went up of "what a fucking prima donna" and the like as Baxter's deputy studied the boss's chin.

"He hit me, he hit me," Baxter kept saying.

And then Torment came back in, walking fast, straight in my direction. The Canadian was still trying to work out what had happened.

"That man just hit that other man," said one of the children, clearly a Rhodes scholar in the making.

Torment was waving to the deskers as if he were the Duchess of York.

"Thanks guys, that was great," he said. "Sorry about the bit of aggro, boss. Not in my nature. No hard feelings."

He said this without bothering to try to find out where Baxter was. Torment reached my desk and stopped.

"Apologies for the other night. The party and all that. And thanks for your help. Don't look at me. Bit of stress. Understand you've got a couple of lines. Let's shake."

I was looking out the window at a Star Ferry slowing down to avoid colliding with another tourist junk with fake sails and extended my arm in the direction I thought Torment was standing. We shook.

"Do I know you?" Torment asked.

"Yes, Chris. You do know me."

"Halfords?"

"Yes."

"Good heavens. Thought the name was familiar. Well, so be it."

He marched back towards the door. Someone clapped again and Torment maddeningly acknowledged the applause.

I TURNED TO MY SCREEN and called up a thirty-line story from Jakarta. Not the usual fare. A car had plunged from the sixth floor of a twenty-floor office block on to the road below.

"I'll take the Indonesia car story," I called over to Fagin, who was the morning acting duty editor.

"All yours I, but it'll need some explaining. I mean, what was he doing up there?"

"About thirty-five miles per hour?"

I picked up the phone and hit the speed dial to the Jakarta bureau. I was aware of a girl standing just out of sight to my right.

"Hello there," I said. "Can I help you?"

The girl raised a notebook and pen grasped in her hands.

"I've come to interview you, if I may. For my school project."

I put down the phone softly. The girl, a pretty Eurasian with long hair, streaks of sunny blond among the brown, was shifting from foot to foot, pulling at a corner of the notebook, looking from side to side and twitching her nose.

"You've come to interview me? What kind of interview?"

The girl shrugged her shoulders. "I recognise that man who caused the fight," she said. "He's an old actor."

"You're right. He's a *very* old actor. A very foolish old actor, if you want my opinion. What's your name?"

"Amanda."

"Well, Amanda, how can I help?"

"What's he doing here? Why does he think he is so important? Why did he hit that man?"

"All good questions. I think actors tend to think very highly of themselves. Between you and me, I think that man is a complete idiot." I winked. "But you want to ask me about my job, I believe."

"Don't journalists think very highly of themselves? That's what my teacher says. Miss Pizza."

"Your teacher is called Miss Pizza?"

"Not her real name, silly. She says that what all journalists really want is to be in show business, but they can't because they're not good enough at anything, and that we shouldn't let any of you touch us in a million years. She says that today, in particular, we shouldn't let any of you come within spitting distance."

"Hadley, any luck on the car window death plunge?" This was Fagin.

"I'm on it."

I turned back to the girl. "I don't think your Miss Pizza has a very high opinion of journalists. She must be married to one."

"No. She's a miss but very pretty. She's very thin and you're meant to ask me now if she's crispy but that doesn't make me laugh. If you don't mind, can I have your name card, please? Miss Pizza said not to ask any question I don't have to, and if you give me your name card I won't have to ask you what your name is or how you spell it or what your job is."

"That is very sensible thinking. A very good first move." I handed over my card.

"Thank you. We were also asked to think outside the box but I don't really know what that means. I think it has something to do with asking different sorts of questions. Not the usual ones."

"I think that's exactly what it means. Unless we're talking about pizza boxes. Ha ha."

Fagin shouted over: "Hadley, CNN have the auto pilot plummet story. Just FYI."

"Thanks, Fagin. No rush." Then to Amanda: "Where were we?" Amanda didn't laugh at the pizza box joke.

"You work in a box," she said. "This office is a sort of a box."

"Well we can go outside it, if you like."

"No need to take it so literally, thank you very much. Miss Pizza has taught us what literally means. Here will do. I thought I'd ask you an either-or question, if that's okay."

"You're not going to ask me about my job?"

"Miss Pizza says my story mustn't be boring."

"Oh."

"So here goes, if that's okay."

"Okay."

"Which would you prefer?"

"Go on."

"Which would you prefer: to have to shower in puke-green nail polish every day for the rest of your life..."

"Puke-green nail polish?"

"Hold on. Or be in the boringest, boringest orchestra in the world and everyone throws food at you, like cucumber cups with low-fat yoghurt inside? And when you go to the bathroom, you have to go in your pants."

I looked at the girl's face. She appeared deadly serious. So where did this mischief spring from? Fagin, from across the room, shoulders hunched and arms extended, was giving me his impersonation of a car plunging out of an office window.

"That's the choice?"

"That's it."

I tapped my fingers on the desk. "Look, are you taking the p...?"

"Piss?"

"What?"

"That's what you were going to ask me. Am I taking the piss."

"I was not. I would not use that kind of language with a... How old are you?"

"Twelve."

"With a twelve-year-old. I was going to ask you if you were taking the..."

"Polygraph test?"

"Polygraph test?"

"It's a test to see if you are lying."

"I know what a polygraph test is."

"My teacher, Miss Pizza..."

"Look," I said too loudly, turning a few heads. I leant towards the girl and whispered: "Enough about bloody Miss Pepperoni Pizza."

"Not funny. My teacher, Miss Pizza, says all journalists are liars."

"Enough."

"In fact, she says all men are liars. It's a song she likes. By Nick Lowe. He's an old man like you and she plays that song again and again. What's your answer?" Amanda looked at my card. "Mr Arnold."

"I'm a very busy man. I want you to go away."

"Is it true you spend your whole day sitting at your desk? That's what another old man told me. Don't they give you any time to go out and play?"

"Play? *Play?* This is a serious business."

"Hadley," Fagin shouted. "The Citroen suicide. What's the status?"

"It's coming!"

"Don't you know what play means?"

"Piss off. What do you want from me?"

Amanda beamed. "Now you're really annoyed."

"Look," I snarled. "I'll take the orchestra and the cucumber sandwich nonsense if you promise you'll go away."

"Good choice. The nail polish my mum uses really stinks. And you can't get it off no matter how hard you try. On nails you can't get it off, and in your hair.... Eeeuw. And imagine trying to get it off your..."

"Enough. What's your intro going to be?"

"What's an intro?"

"Your first paragraph. For the story you're going to write."

"Well it would be that you don't want to be a journalist after all, but that what you really, really want is to be in a boring orchestra and poo in your pants."

"That's not what I said."

"Yes you did. I just asked you."

"But it was a choice, smarty-pants. A really silly choice, if you don't mind my saying."

"And you chose to be in the boringest, boringest orchestra."

"It's most boring, not boringest."

"Well, you should know."

"Look, go away."

"I'm going to tell on you to Miss Pizza."

"You dare."

"I'm going to tell her you used the P-word."

"I'll deny it."

"And the F-word."

I pulled open my drawer and pulled out a tape recorder, switching it on in one easy motion before slamming it on the desk in front of the girl. Again, a few heads turned.

"See that red light?" I said. "That red light means this recorder has been on all this time and I have *proof* of what I did and didn't say."

"You just turned it on."

"Prove it."

Amanda picked it up off the desk. "It hasn't got a tape in it, silly."

I snatched it back and looked at the little window. Smartypants was right.

"And why do you use an old-fashioned gadget like this when you could use a digital recorder?" she asked. "Is it because you don't understand new technology?" I just stared at her. "Is it because you are too old?"

"What do you want?"

"What?"

"What do you want? What can I give you to leave me alone?"

"Can I choose anything?"

"Within reason."

Amanda slowly reached forward and prised the tape recorder from my hand, a big smile on her face. She raised her eyebrows, asking if this was within reason. I shooed her away and she skipped happily towards the door.

CHAPTER SIX

HONG KONG'S FOREIGN Correspondents' Club was made famous by John le Carre's 'The Honourable Schoolboy', in which a bunch of old hacks sit around during a typhoon flicking screwed-up napkins into a wine rack. It doesn't sound very exciting, but the FCC is not a very exciting place. At least back then, in the mid-1970s, it was a club for foreign correspondents, on the thirteenth floor of a building where the gents overlooked the harbour. Hong Kong was still a listening post for what was going on over the border in inscrutable China and a favoured R&R bolthole from Vietnam. Shrubs had its own dedicated phone with a flashing red light in case anything was happening back in the office. Now, housed in a colonial-era brick and stucco building which once served as a cold storage depot for a dairy company, the FCC is full of lawyers, fund managers and middle-aged women wearing lots of jewellery, with the odd, old hack propping up the bar, pressing his claim that he was one of the characters in 'The Honourable Schoolboy'.

"That scene when they're flicking screwed up napkins into the wine rack? Remember? Remember? Well, I was there at the time. Le Carre saw me. That was me."

The rehearsals went badly. They lasted from six in the morning until eight in the evening and all for the one scene at the FCC's grand main bar which made me feel as though I were sitting inside a huge, stale, lemon-coloured wedding cake.

Torment was throwing tantrums. Adolf Lee was charming. I

tried the one line I had to speak.

"Here, where have all the babes gone? Do you... want a crisp?"

Adolf Lee's aide forced a laugh. "Hadley, please, you must relax. What's with the 'do you... want a crisp'? The pause? That's not how we want it. You're not questioning the who or the what. It's an instinctive, meaningless courtesy. It's flat. It's 'do you want a crisp'. There is no question mark."

"Do you want a crisp."

"That's it."

"There's no question mark. Do you want a crisp."

"That's much better. And don't forget, you are glum."

"Glum. Do you want a crisp."

So far so good. Then came the real thing. Seventeen takes. I could not relax. I was sweating and stinking the whole bar out – stinking up the whole movie. And Torment had basically said nothing to me. He came up once and offered me some toffee, but that was it. James, the guy playing Magnus, was a complete prick. Adolf Lee, not sitting on a bus this time but on what looked like a tennis umpire's chair in my favourite corner of the bar, said: "Okay everyone. Let's do it. Let's try it one more time."

"Do you want a crisp. Here, where have all the babes gone? Do you want a crisp. I think I've got it this time. I think I've got it."

"Pull your finger out, Hadley Arnold," Torment said at last.

"Okay, Hadley." This was Adolf Lee. "Chris, James, are you ready?"

Torment heaved a sigh and nodded. He leant against the bar.

"Okay, bar noises, background conversation. Traffic and... action!"

Torment started going through the motions. Put on his pained Englishman look. Cut short a couple of smirks – an annoying habit he had stolen from Dustin Hoffman. Played with a bar mat.

"There's something they're not telling us, Magnus," he said, frowning. "I've been racking my brains..."

"It's the new regime, Scott," Magnus said faultlessly. "It's something we're going to have to get used to."

I admired their presence. And I was convinced I could match their professionalism with my one, strategically important line. I breathed in deeply and launched:

"Here, where have all the crisps gone?"

Torment slapped the palm of his hand down hard on the bar.

"That's it," he said.

"Babes! Where have all the babes gone!"

"That's not good enough and that's it," Torment said. "And don't look at me." He slapped the bar again. "Adolf, James, time is precious to me. Time is precious to you. We are expensive people. We don't need – *I* don't need – to work with... *arses* like this."

"It wasn't deliberate," I protested. "And I'm not an arse."

"Yes you are."

"Guys, guys, let's move along," Adolf Lee said. "It's almost there. Just a little hiccup. Chris, you are so real."

"Thanks, Adolf. I felt it. But that was the seventeenth take. For a piss-poor scene that anyone could do in their sleep..."

"Don't worry, Hadley," Adolf said. "We'll get there."

"Can't we just scrap the line?" This was Torment.

"Scrap the line?" I cried. "Exit glum man in bar?"

"It has to have an edge," Torment said looking at the floor. "You don't know what I'm talking about but it's not working. Even when you get the line right. It has to be harder."

"That's what he said last night."

"Oh go away, you feckless fool. Shoo, shoo."

"We're not scrapping the line," Adolf ruled. "Take five everybody."

Another two takes and it was in the can and I felt on top of the world as I left the FCC. Two Bangladeshi security men were standing at the open door. Security men were outside the door too. They were all over the place, and out of uniform.

"I'm in the movies," I said to one, a big smile on my face.

"Congratulations, sir."

So this was how it felt to be in the movies. It was a huge lift. Imagine this magnified a hundred times, a thousand times, if you were a major star and had hundreds of lines, not just one. It would transform your life. No wonder Chris Torment was so... unbearable. It was instant fame, a drug I wouldn't be able to get enough of and I would become an arrogant piece of shit like... Chris Torment.

"Get in, Hadley," said Joe.

The stretch limo had pulled up as I marched along with my thoughts, striding up the street like an SS officer on an airstrip called to the phone. The back door opened and I looked down at a sulking Panda Koo. Her lips were too good to be true. In Chinese literature, they would be described as persimmons. I didn't have a clue what a persimmon was but suspected it was something lush and sensuous and unavailable in the Fens.

"Hello, Hadley," she said.

I climbed in and sat opposite her. My eyes rested on the lips. "Hello Panda," I said. "You know my name."

Joe put a hand on Panda's knee and smiled at me. Next to him was a bucket of champagne standing on a magazine with a picture of Cary Grant on the cover.

"Well, that went very well," he said. "In the end. You know Panda, right?"

"Yes, we've met a few times on the set." Panda smiled briefly. I was breathing heavily. "I blew my lines, Joe. Or rather, my line. But I got there in the end. How do you know it went well?"

"Can I pour you some champagne?" Panda said.

"I think I can help you," Joe said.

"No, I can manage."

"Not you, Panda. I mean I think I can help Hadley."

"Help me do what?"

"Help me do what?" Joe mimicked. "I can help you do this, I can help you do that. What was that film, now? Back in the

Fens?"

" 'Great Expectations'."

"Right. 'Great Expectations'. I checked it out in my records. It never got made. Boy, it was a long time ago and I wasn't directly involved." Joe was playing with his ear. "I was just in the neighbourhood. But the director got run over and broke his legs and one of the actors came down with botulism. Both on the same day."

"Really?"

"Really. I checked the records."

"I'm surprised our paper didn't pick up on it. Broke *both* his legs?"

"That's what the records say. They weren't explicit. Your friend Torment's movie debut was delayed somewhat."

"Extraordinary. What records might they be, then?"

Joe declared the subject closed with another laugh and a dismissive wave of his hand. "Listen Hadley, if you don't mind, I'd like to spend the rest of the drive in silence. I love this drive. Basically, I love Hong Kong. Panda understands. You don't mind?"

"Of course not."

I briefly caught Panda's glistening eyes and detected a faint sneer. The car swished down towards Central and then turned up Cotton Tree Drive, Magazine Gap Road, Peak Road, a different harbour view at every turn. A few more weeks and mist would cover the hills and apartment blocks and the smell of wet leaves would remind me of my childhood in England. An unexpected rush of collywobbles accompanied the thought of how many typhoons Adolf Lee would feature in this Hong Kong movie. There had to be at least one. And at least one fire in a floating restaurant and a stock market collapse. And probably some bollocks in the lobby of the Peninsula Hotel.

The car turned on to Harlech Road, a narrow track that circles the Peak. This was for walkers and joggers – no cars allowed except for those needing access to the weather-beaten blocks of old flats and the occasional isolated houses sitting on the most sought-after real estate in the world, fenced off with barbed wire and notices warning of big dogs.

You start off on Harlech Road, passing waterfalls and stone cliffs and hills iced with cement to stop rocks falling on your right. The cement turns dark green with lichen within weeks. On the left is jungle full of Burmese pythons with views down to Aberdeen and out across the South China Sea. Then the track starts edging round the Peak (the name changes to Lugard Road) and the hum of the harbour grows until you are looking down on the lights of the boats and the construction and traffic and people playing tennis in fancy clubs squeezed in between the high-rise buildings. Time it right, and the sun will be setting on the final stretch back to where you started at the Peak Tram. The whole city, by this time, has turned pink.

I knew Harlech Road very well, but the limo turned down a drive into unexplored territory. There were rhododendron bushes down each side and expanses of lawn beyond. At the edge of a neglected hard tennis court with no net, the car turned into another drive and stopped outside a white bungalow. I was amazed – too amazed to say anything. Before I could collect my thoughts, I found myself sitting in a long drawing room where Joe was tinkering with bottles and glasses. I was aware that Panda had somehow been dismissed. Just like in the movies.

"She's beautiful, isn't she? I'm getting you a Scotch, no ice, if that's okay."

"Sure. Yes. Please. Panda, you mean? Yes, she is. Stunning."

"Beautiful. And colourful. Extraordinary story." Joe gave me my drink, sat down and loosened his tie.

"Extraordinary?"

"She came third in one of the Hong Kong pageants. Miss Great Ass or something. Caught the eye of a young Macau gangster who plied her with roses and a fast car and had her working on her back within three weeks, servicing Cantonese movie celebrities."

I shuffled in my seat. "You're kidding, right?"

"No, I'm not kidding. But she liked it. She thought it was challenging, fun and the lifestyle she got by doing it was straight out of the teen magazines she used to read on the Star Ferry. She found bit parts in Cantonese soaps which went down big on the mainland and then got a Canto pop record deal. One thing led to another. We found her. I found her. Good English. Here she is. Cheers."

"I seem to remember there was some scandal about a boy-friend found dead near one of those weekend getaways at Big Wave Bay."

"That so?" Joe said. "Don't recall."

"The newspapers said he was involved in illegal road racing and gambling. Probably a Triad killing. Maybe it was the Macau gangster?"

"I'll ask her about that one. But don't believe everything you read."

"No, you're right."

"I mean, I don't have to tell *you*, right? About the crap news-papers print."

"Right."

Joe fidgeted, downed his drink. "I read the news today," he said. "Boy oh boy."

I swallowed. Again the image of the Cadillac written on the wing mirror slipped into my head. "So who are you guys?"

"Hah! You like that line. 'Butch Cassidy and the Sundance Kid'... William Goldman script. The man in the white hat. De-liberate repetition to reinforce the mystery. There's no need for such dramatics. I'll try to explain a little. On the condition that you keep it quiet."

"Okay."

"My first bit of advice to you is... don't be such a pup."

"What?"

"It's something I've noticed about you. You hold on to this Englishness, this aloofness. You think you're great and sophisticated with a superior slant on life. You think you're better than all other nationalities and races. But you're not. You're an observer, a sneerer, but you don't actually *do* anything. You don't take any risks. You don't raise your head above the parapet. The people in the world out there, if they knew you, if they *knew* you, would despise you."

I was silent but preparing a protest. I tried to summon up a bit of anger. "It isn't deliberate," I said.

"Don't mind me. It's a little rant, that's all. It's a little speech I've made to many Brits before you. The modern Westerner is inherently weak. Too much too easy. And no religion too. But let's talk about this movie you're involved in. It may be taking off. Don't worry about needing ten, twenty takes in any scene – that's how this business works. People forget their lines, people lose their tempers, people forget they don't have divine rights. This movie's perfect for you."

"I don't know. I don't get on with Chris Torment. I was at school..."

"You were at school with him, I know."

"How did you know?"

"He treated you shamelessly."

"He did."

"And he had intimate relations with your sister."

"Intimate relations with my sister? What do you mean my sister?"

"Well..."

"How do you know? I don't believe you."

"I can show you the video."

"You have a video of Torment having intimate relations with my sister?"

"No, not really." Joe stood up to forestall any protest. "But I'm not lying to you, Hadley. Let me put it this way: this movie project that you are involved in is gaining momentum."

"But what do you mean, intimate relations?"

"Just forget about that for now. Listen to me. This movie is gaining momentum, which is bad. It's good for Adolf Lee and it will be good presumably for your friend Torment. But it's not good for the people I represent."

"Who are they?" Intimate relations?

Joe pulled down a book from a shelf next to a huge, flat television and threw it into my lap. It was 'Mr Tony's Book of Movies', with the words 'Best Seller' splashed across the front.

"Think of a Chris Torment movie and look it up."

I opened the book. "I can't think of one off the top of my head."

"Well that is a major part of the problem, you stuck-up Brit. Let me help. 'Northwest Frontier'." I searched for the page. "Four stars for the best. I have yet to find a Chris Torment movie that has scored anything."

I read: " 'Northwest Frontier'. Relentless, moribund 'action' flick set on the northern frontier of India. Laughingly inappropriate remake of a 1959 British classic starring Lauren Bacall and Kenneth More. Chris Torment, in the part originally played by More, wears extraordinary khaki shorts."

"Look up another."

My memory leapt back like a wet salmon and I happily turned to 'Silent and a Stranger'. "Chris Torment limps around the screen sulking like a six-year-old when he should be striding and rampaging. The film's only saving grace is that, as the stranger, he is more often than not silent."

"Try 'Othello'."

I sniggered and found the page quickly. "Chris Torment manages to make Iago as devious as a two-day-old puppy."

"I rest my case."

"I'm sorry, but I think I am missing the point."

"You Brits are so protective of your actors," Joe said from the end of the room. "You have some mighty fine actors, don't get me wrong. But you let people like Torment get away with murder. All he is, is a pretty face. He's not a song-and-dance man, he's not funny, he's got about as much personality as a coffee table and yet he's paraded around like Larry Olivier. I mean, what is it about this guy?"

"There's nothing you have said that I don't agree with. I hate everything about the man. But I still don't see the point."

Joe sat down and slowly placed his elbows on his knees.

"This here's the problem," he said. "There's speculation that Torment may take over as the next James Bond. The guy is pushing forty-five, for God's sake."

"Go on."

"We're talking James Bond here. There is a heritage that has to be protected. Resurrected and protected."

"So you..."

"...want to stop him. Yes. As I said, this movie, 'Love in Hong Kong' or whatever, is likely to make waves, and Torment may find himself washed along with all the hype and come out of it looking terrific. Now you and I both know that he isn't terrific at anything. He's useless."

I paused. I felt as though I was in a vacuum. "So who are you guys?"

"You'll never know. The only reason I'm letting you in on this much is because you'll never know the full story. You thought you had stumbled on a story all those years ago. You don't know how big it actually is. You thought we were movie producers, and that's kind of what we are, but without the billing. The key point is that we insist on integrity. The only reason I'm telling you so much is because of what Torment has done to you and what you may be able to do for us, as part of this film. Just remember that no one would believe someone like you if you were to talk about it. And you would never get the chance to. People have tried before."

"Tried what?"

"To spill the beans. To expose us."

"You mean... Wait, are you threatening me?"

"We have a lot of money. That's how I know so much about you. That's how I know about your sister, whom Torment courted and seduced when she was seventeen."

" 'Courted and seduced'? 'Whom'? What language are you speaking? What are you talking about? Does Adolf Lee or Torment know about you? Who you are?"

"Not specifically. They suspect people like us exist. As it happens, I am helping Adolf in another capacity with this film. He is using some of my back catalogue."

"Back catalogue?"

"Some of my archive material. I film things, you see. All the time. I am filming even as we speak." Joe nodded my head towards the top of the far wall where I saw a tiny black security camera sunk into a recess. "I have footage of the strangest moments."

"Does Panda know about you? About your organisation?"

"No."

"The assassination attempt?"

Joe shrugged his shoulders.

"Are you political?"

"I don't know what that means. If you're asking do we try to bring down governments, then the answer is no. What we do is art, basically. Yeah. Basically, it's art."

"So what do you want me to do? Why don't you just take him aside and tell him? Or break his legs or something." A penny dropped. "Back in the Fens, 'Great Expectations'. You said..."

"Violence tends to be a last resort in these situations. It's part of our code of conduct. We like to do things with, how should I say, theatrical flourish." Joe sat down excitedly and leant forward on his knees again. "You know the first movie I was involved in?"

" 'Mary Poppins'?"

"Hah! You are trying to be funny. But you are close, you feck-less boy who weeps and wails. Julie Andrews was involved. 'My Fair Lady'... We wanted her, not Audrey Hepburn. We wanted her beautiful singing voice. Wouldn't it be lo-ver-ly, we thought. It was my first movie and we failed. But before we failed, you know what we did? To try to dissuade her?" I shook my head. "We sent her flowers. Eliza Doolittle. She's the flower girl, see. So we sent her flowers, every hour of every day, signing off as an obsessive fan."

"A flower stalker."

"Well, there were wild threats enclosed in the little envelopes that came with the flowers. But she didn't take the hint."

"Why should it be so important? Who gives a shit?"

Joe appeared not to hear. "Another important part of our work, my work, is to keep things clean. I'm not a big fan of bad language or bad behaviour. It's lazy."

"You're having me on, aren't you? This is all some put-up job."

Joe wagged his finger. "No, no. You are more likely a put-up job."

"You mean you're telling me you are some sort of CIA censor? What could have been so offensive about 'Great Expectations', for heaven's sake? How many F-words did Miss Havisham have in mind? How many times was Pip planning to give Magwitch one? And what could be wrong with Audrey Hepburn?"

"Well, she had to be dubbed, for a start. By Marni Nixon. Did you know that? None of it is important now and I can't remember all the details. I also don't want to stray from the project at hand because time waits for no man and I want you to think about James Bond and what you could do, and what you would want to do, in order to stop Torment."

"Time waits for no man? For heaven's sake. Can I have another drink?"

Joe waved an arm in the direction of the cabinet. "I'll make it easy for you. Think about actors you would like to play Bond. Dead or alive. Just for fun. Pierce Brosnan was never my choice, by the way, but I wasn't involved in the franchise at the time."

I poured myself a whisky and looked at Joe. How could he be so earnest? "I always thought Patrick McGoohan..."

"Brilliant! Now you are beginning to feel the passion of the role and for the job in hand. McGoohan would have been an excellent James Bond. Up there with Connery. He had the coldness and the brutality. All Brosnan and Moore had was charm. I've told the team that the actor who plays 007 must be dark, hard and brutal. He cannot look like a guy who has soft hands or wears an earring or uses hairspray. And he's gotta have a sense of humour. It's like, in news, I believe you have a saying that you want to throw a story forward? To focus on what happens next rather than what's happened? Well, it's the same here. We start again."

"Do you know who it's going to be?"

"Who?"

"The next Bond."

"I don't want to give too much away but we've narrowed it down and we know who we want. I can tell you that it won't be another Australian or an American. Clive Owen's too boring. Ewan McGregor's too... Ewan McGregor. David Beckham passed a lot of the tests."

"You have to be kidding. He's not dark."

"He has looks going for him. Getting old, though."

"Can he act?"

"Look, forget about David Beckham. What's important is that you're really beginning to think about this part."

"And David Beckham wears an earring, I believe. He may wear two. You wear an earring."

"Yes, but I am not a contender. Are you going to help us out?"

"I haven't a clue. I find you a bit scary, to tell you the truth.

What do you want me to do?"

"Well, you've got options. You're a newsman. Isn't there something provisional you could do? Can you write something?"

"You mean make something up?"

"Sure. Put some innuendo out there. Get people worrying about his moral fibre, or – even better – his sexuality. You Brits are all so hung up about homosexuals. Get them talking about a gay James Bond contender. It's perfect."

"Can't you lay off the Brits for one minute? You think I can just go around making up stories?"

"Isn't that what you do?"

"I don't understand. You say you have these high ideals about the movies, but it seems like you'd stoop pretty low to achieve them. You are completely amoral."

The shadow of a smile crossed Joe's face. It went away as quickly as it had come and left the impression that he believed he had scored a point.

"You didn't answer the question."

"What question?"

Joe got up from his chair and walked slowly around behind me, like a school headmaster invigilating an exam. "The question I just asked. The one about whether or not you make up stories."

"You think we can just make up stories? The whole point of the news agency business is that we get it right and are seen getting it right. Or else no one would ever use us. Everything is sourced. "

"So every quote is word for word legit?"

"Of course it is! You obviously don't know much about news. How long do you think we would be in business if we made up quotes?"

I felt one of my lapses of concentration coming on. I drifted back to my days on the Sotobech Sentinel and a fabricated Women's Institute report sent to a rival paper about a handicraft afternoon in which the only materials at hand for each member were a cucumber, two onions and lots of aluminium foil.

"Sorry?" I realised Joe was speaking to me in the present. Twenty years later. In a house on the Peak in Hong Kong.

"I said, what about that double happiness Valentine's Day shit?"

"I'm sorry?"

I racked my brain and resented having to. I had produced sixty lines the day St Valentine's Day coincided with the Chinese equivalent in the lunar calendar. I had had to go out to flower shops and find out how much bouquets of roses were selling for, how much a romantic dinner for two would set you back at the Peninsula Hotel. I had to ask people in the street if love could conquer all.

"Does this day have special significance for you, being St Valentine's Day and the Chinese equivalent?" I had asked one unsuspecting young Chinese couple as they stepped off a tram.

"Ah?"

"Do you think it's extra romantic, poignant, because of the two days being on the same day?"

"Ah?"

A few hours later I was banging out my story.

"Love is a many splendoured thing, or so the saying goes, and St Valentine's Day meant double happiness for Hong Kong's young and restless on Tuesday as East met West in an alignment of the stars."

Ah?

"Well, what about it?" I asked.

"Did you think that was a good story?"

"No, it was a piece of rubbish. But it was a harmless piece of rubbish. No one was expecting an in-depth survey. No one's credibility was at stake. Certainly not mine. It was a fun story about young lovers!"

"What do you know about young lovers?"

"It was an extended caption to go with a picture. We call them slice-of-life stories. Stand-alone stories to accompany a picture.

It wasn't the Nuremberg trials."

"Well I want to put your idiot friend Chris Torment on some kind of trial."

"I am not going to manufacture stories."

"So write what you see. I know how you feel about Torment. Don't try to pretend to me that there is such a thing as an objectively written story. Boy, I know more about your business than you do." Joe leant forward and picked up a copy of a Hong Kong newspaper from the table. "The first story I see... and it backs up my case completely."

"What case?"

"Oh look, it's a Shrubs story. What a surprise."

"What story?"

"Let me read the beginning. It's great." Joe cleared his throat and began to read:

" *'An Indonesian taxi driver took a fateful wrong turn at the top of a sixth-floor car park in downtown Jakarta and ended up in a no-stopping zone in the street below'.*"

I swallowed.

"He took a wrong turn," Joe said. "How *fateful*. He landed in a no-stopping zone. How *funny*. Let's read the quote to tell us how the story is backed up. *'It's the sixth floor of a downtown building and this is the sixth time this has happened in six weeks,' a local newspaper said.'*"

"That's what the newspaper said."

"It's not even a person being quoted. It's an unnamed local newspaper. And you believe it? Of course you don't. What is the matter with your Jakarta reporter? Or reporters? How many of them are there?"

I kept quiet. I wasn't going to own up to having rewritten the whole thing.

"Clearly Shrubs has some artistic licence," Joe said. "But I'm just telling you to write what you see. Maybe Torment will take a wrong turn out of a helicopter and you will see that."

"You're kidding, I hope."

"Or maybe he goes back to this gunman Chen's home in Sri Lanka as a public relations exercise, and combines it with a visit to a monsoon disaster region. And Shrubs sends you along."

"Why would they?"

"Because I will arrange it."

"Do you control my company too?"

"Well, of course not. But I think we could arrange something. Something really imaginative."

"Shrubs has stopped covering showbiz VIPs on aid missions. They cause more problems than they are worth with their fancy hotels, round-the-clock security, women delivered to their rooms. It's all grandstanding and pretty evil."

"Just write what you see."

CHAPTER SEVEN

BAXTER CALL ME into his office the next day.

"Go home and pack your bags."

"Where am I going?"

"Sri Lanka. Storm aid. Appears your mate Chris Torment is going on a mercy mission and we want you to cover it."

"Whose idea was this?"

"What does it matter? Part of it was my idea. We can't just let the floods and mudslides fall off the radar screen."

"I thought we had stopped covering showbiz farts wasting people's time and resources."

"Well, we've just started again."

For the makers of the film, the idea was to make the most of the publicity over the shooting attempt while they waited for the critical spring mist to appear over the Peak. A concerned Chris Torment was going in to assess the monsoon reconstruction and look grave in an ample number of photo ops. He was going to the heart of Macho, apparently a dangerous place, and to be sympathetic with everyone he met. Who knows, maybe he would forgive the ill-starred Chen when he returned to Hong Kong? The film people also wanted to patch up relations with Shrubs in the wake of Torment's assault on Baxter. Joe just wanted to see Torment discredited. And what did I want? I wanted an easy, short trip, during which stories would write themselves, with bylines flying around the major newspapers of the world. Screwing up Torment's life would be an added bonus.

The Sri Lankan Chinese group's attempt on Torment's life created good publicity for itself for a while. Serious newspapers around the world, used to years of bloody civil war on the tiny, tear-shaped island once called Ceylon, were sending reporters into Jaffna and desperately trying to find someone Chinese. The Shrubs Beijing bureau got a comment from the Foreign Ministry saying merely that China did not interfere in the internal affairs of a sovereign nation like Sri Lanka. Off the record, Chinese officials said they had never heard of the group.

The agency was also trying to locate its Jaffna stringer who had been out of contact with head office for months. He was a fifty-one-year-old Portuguese priest with the very English name of Waverly who wore flowers in his hair. He had a drinking problem and was said to live with a teenage Tamil girl.

Hong Kong did a sidebar on my involvement in the film, my presence of mind during the botched assassination and my "long-time friendship" with Torment stretching back to school.

I had been allowed to visit Chen, the gunman, twice in Stanley prison, where he was awaiting formal charges. Chen ran off a list of Torment's films that he thought were awful and patronising and I couldn't disagree.

"It's not just his acting. He is totally ignorant."

"And racist, I suspect."

A bit of prompting there. Joe would disapprove. Fuck off, Joe.

"Totally racist. He makes the world cringe with embarrassment. He is self-promotional and crass."

Boy oh boy. I was used to having to draw the usable quote out of interviewees, but this guy was a natural.

"So you don't like Chris Torment?"

"Like I said, he makes the world cringe with embarrassment."

"Is it because he's English?"

"The English can be very arrogant in their modalities."

"And is this personal? Or are you speaking on behalf of your organisation?"

"The Democratic Association for the Liberation of Jaffna Chinese."

"That's the one. I'm afraid I had never heard of it."

Chen looked surprised. "You'd never heard of it?"

"No. Sorry."

"And that's another reason."

"What's another reason?"

"The ignorance. He called us Muslim extremists."

"What? Really?"

"We are not Muslim extremists. I am a scientologist."

Chen had seen a television interview in which Chris Torment had branded all separatist groups in Asia as Muslim extremists. The main separatist group in Sri Lanka at the time was Tamil and most Tamils are Hindu. But then, why would anyone want to ask Chris Torment about separatist groups in Asia? You might just as well ask him to translate Beowulf into Spanish.

"Well, Mr Chen, can you tell me a bit about your group and what it hopes to achieve?"

"Which group?"

"Your group."

Chen stood up. "The answer is easy. We are democratic and we expect liberation..."

"...Of the Jaffna Chinese. Yes, I know that. But can you tell me a bit *more*? How many of you are there, for instance?"

"We do not think a cause can be measured in numbers."

"Of course not. But if there were tens of thousands of you, it would help. I guess the population of Jaffna is well short of a million."

"This is not painting by numbers."

"No. But you are expecting a Chinese homeland in Jaffna, which already is a tiny, tiny place. Tamils consider Jaffna their homeland too."

Chen puffed up his cheeks. "Chris Torment..."

"Yes?"

"...is..."

"Yes?" I had an idea. Tell me he's a coward. Forget Joe's homophobic nonsense and say he's a coward without any prompting from me. Who ever heard of a *cowardly* James Bond. "Chris Torment is what?"

"...a prick. Do you think they will put me away for years and years?"

"I doubt it very much. Nothing actually happened. But tell me more about how you feel about Chris Torment. How do you think he behaved that night? I guess..." Fuck off, Joe. "...I guess he was pretty brave."

"*Brave?*"

"Don't you think so? Pretty courageous the way he stood up to you."

"Ha! Are we talking about the same night? Chris Torment? *Brave?*" I was poised, pen over paper. The man with the golden quote. "He wasn't *brave*. The man is the personification of cowardice." Yes! "His manhood was put on the line and it was found wanting." Perfection! Time to wrap this up discreetly.

"Mr Chen?"

"Yes?"

"Gotta go."

Shrubs ran the story, which was thin on detail about the DALJC, but beautifully fat in innuendo about Torment's character, or lack thereof. I clapped and rubbed my hands together when I saw how the tawdry London tabloid I had laid out the 007 piece for years earlier had used the news – and given me a byline.

"Would-be assassin brands would-be Bond a coward."

Adolf Lee was furious and threatened legal action.

"I think we should talk," Torment said on the phone the same day.

"What about?"

"Well, this man, actually. This Chen fellow."

"I'm just doing my job."

"But look at what he's saying, man. Look at what you're quoting him as saying."

"Yeah? So?"

"I'm not blaming you. But things have been going badly wrong for me lately. My reputation's at stake."

CHRIS TORMENT was suddenly everywhere in the Hong Kong media and in Hong Kong. There was a picture of him in the South China Morning Post handing out school awards. Coming into town by train, I had seen a picture of him on the back page of someone's Chinese newspaper holding a large fish. Every night, one of the channels would have a report of where Torment had been shooting that day. I had seen him on location three times – the first time outside the backpacker warren of Chungking Mansions, then just around the corner in front of the colonial-era Peninsula Hotel (why can't film people leave the Peninsula Hotel alone?) and then at the Mariners' Club, the cheapest club in town with a deep, clean and heated pool overlooked by towering trees. It was Hong Kong 1960s style, and one of my favourite haunts.

"Why did you let him in here?" I whined to the English manager, a stout former sailor from Kent.

"What do you mean, why did I let him in here?"

"I mean what business did he have coming in here?"

"He's making a movie, isn't he? What have you got against him anyway? He seemed a right gent."

"Close, but no cigar."

"What?"

I sat alone at a poolside table and watched a Macau jetfoil captain teach his new girlfriend how to dive while he patted her bottom a lot. I was drinking beer and smoking and, to my astonishment, talking to myself. I caught myself at it and stopped and turned around to see if anyone was within earshot. A 360-degree scowl. The girl learning how to dive was giving me glances.

"Who are those guys?" a voice on the radio said. Ah-Dai, the old Cantonese waiter behind the hatch, had switched to an English-language station. "The stress is important. It's not who are those *guys* or who are *those* guys, but... who *are* those guys?"

"You've got to be kidding," I said to no one.

"Paul Newman in 'Butch Cassidy and the Sundance Kid'."

"That is correct! Too easy, I suspect, for most of you movie-goers out there. If you've just tuned in, welcome to 'Name That Movie!'. We're at the fun bit of the show where I give our inter-viewee quotes out of the movies, as short as possible, mind, and ask him or her to Name That Movie! I am Frank and when it comes to watching movies, avid is my middle name. It should have been David, but someone forgot the D."

"Go away." I said loudly. The girl fluffed a dive.

"But seriously," the man on the radio said, "'Butch Cassidy' it was, and now I turn again to our star guest Chris Torment..."

"Oh please," I said, putting my head in my hands.

"...who should get this, after that boxing we all saw in that wonderful movie 'The Count of Fire Station Foxtrot'. You real-ly are a count." The presenter laughed. As genuine as a Hong Kong-made Rolex. "No. seriously, Chris, I'm asking. Is it true you're a count?"

"I *was* a count in that movie. I played the count."

"I think it would be safe to leave it there and turn to the quiz movie. Here is your word, Chris. Sorry, two words."

"That's three words."

Laughter from the fuckwit presenter. "I haven't started yet."

"That's four words."

More laughter. Ha, ha, ha. "Chris, don't be a count..." More ribald laughter! "Your *two* words (oh dear, oh dear, breaking down now), your two words... I'll start so I'll finish... The scene is the back seat of a car. I used..."

"...to be a contender. Too easy."

"No, Chris. You're far too good. Humour us. What movie?"

" 'On the Waterfront'."

"Yes! 'On the Waterfront' it is indeed, and that means I shuffle my cards. Here we go. One word. Lovable."

" 'Manchurian Candidate'." This was me. No word from Torment. " 'The Manchurian Candidate'," I said again. "Come on, Chris, you can do this. Laurence Harvey's drunk, he's opening up, pouring his heart out to Sinatra, and he says how lovable he was with his girlfriend, with everyone! Come on!"

"Hadley," ah-Dai the waiter called from the hatch. "Don't make so loud. I bring you another beer and you quieten."

"Lovable," Torment repeated on the radio.

"Like you, Chris," the presenter said. "Everyone loves you in Hong Kong. Tick tock, tick tock. Time waits for no man. Nothing?"

Of course there's nothing. Chris Torment is a hole. He's an empty white paper bag.

"Nothing stirring behind that handsome face?"

I've seen that handsome face and nothing ever stirs behind it. Stupidity stirs *on* it, under the eyes, around the mouth, but nothing behind it.

"Can you give me a clue?" Torment said.

"You crap." This was me again.

"Oh dear, okay. A quick one. It stars Frank Sinatra and Laurence Harvey and it's on the box this week. In fact, tonight. It was on tonight, if this show is aired at its normal time. Considering we recorded this three days ago. So to speak."

" 'Pal Joey'?"

Way too much air time. Someone turn him off.

I had arranged to meet Torment at my local, the Honest Bar, and I arrived early, had a couple of eye-openers and enjoyed a subtle verbal exchange with Maria.

"I'm meeting someone here tonight who's famous."

"Bullshit."

I surveyed that night's clientele. Another New Territories bar owner sat at one of the tables, wearing rings and tattoos and speaking earnestly to a heavily made-up tai tai – a rich Cantonese housewife. A couple of duck farmers sat side-by-side without speaking, one of whom clenched a cigarette between his teeth and was cleaning behind a toenail with a toothpick. His rubber sandals were on the table. At the bar, ten seats away from me, was a gweilo reading a book. I knew this man. Well, I didn't actually know him, but I had seen him many times at the same place at the bar so he knew my face. He was always reading a book, stroking his moustache, never saying a dicky-bird to anyone. He looked a bit like a famous cricketer.

I looked at Maria now and wondered, not for the first time, what she would be like in bed. She had the body of a supermodel (and was as bad-tempered as a supermodel), but never shared it with customers. She was famous for it. She would bar-fine all right, and go to dinners or parties with fee-paying customers. But that was it. No hanky-panky. She was one of a long line of beautiful girls forced to escape the corrupt, feckless Philippines and work in a bar overseas; another Filipina low on her luck.

"Maria?"

"What?" It was a bark, not a question.

"You're beautiful."

Maria had spent ten years in the bars of Hong Kong and the torrent of abuse she could unleash as soon as she had powdered her nose shook the English suits to the core. She had them running for cover, something she had learnt how to do herself in the Manila slum where, as the youngest of eight children, who were beaten by their drunk jeepney driver father, she had spent a lot of time finding places to cower. She came from Smoky Mountain, a giant heap of trash on Manila Bay which literally smoked and burst into flames in different places several times a day as residents hunted through the rubbish for anything they could sell which hadn't been burnt. It was a vision of hell that was hard to match, yet it had its own Easter Parade, with a Miss Smoky Mountain, which Maria won two years in a row.

She rode a float elaborately decorated with trash and icons of the Virgin Mary and a little chimney on top proudly representing the barangay of Smoky Mountain.

Sometimes the family decamped to the narrow stretch of grass and human excrement and dead dogs between the main drag of Roxas Boulevard and Intramuros golf course, where her brothers would poke their noses through the wire fence, offering to retrieve golf balls sliced into the traffic for a peso a go. They would be told by careless, sweating, red-faced whites to piss off several times a day. When it was dark, after eating rice and grey meat from a cauldron, they would sneak under the fence and drop noiselessly into the water hazards to find golf balls, most of them one shot away from being brand new, which they would sell in bags of ten the next day to the same players who lost them.

Maria's three sisters, by the age of eighteen, had found nice-paying jobs in Ermita, which was the main red light district at the time, where servicing one panting westerner would provide the same money their brothers earned in a month by the wire fence. And that was just before lunch. The evening could bring untold riches, but only for a while – once their brothers and father cottoned on, they took all of the money. So the girls went freelance – left home and found a heroin addict of a pimp who took ninety percent of their takings and left them almost as badly off as they had been before, except now they had an affection for shabu, a nasty little drug which made them anybody's without worrying about asking for money.

Maria followed her sisters to Ermita to watch, usually hiding in a doorway below the Spider's Web, a bar where only ugly men and old, rouged women used to come through the doors. She watched her elder sister, Lourdes, put on her makeup and lip-stick and become flirtatious in front of a broken mirror in a filthy toilet. From afar, she watched her on a street corner, swinging languidly around a power pole with live wires stretched across the top. Maria retched, but kept watching, and learnt. What looked like an old man, probably in his mid-thirties, with big, greying hair, smoking a cigarette, came up to Lourdes and spoke a while and looked shifty and kept glancing from side to side.

They walked off together, and the man, wearing a tweed jacket despite the tropical heat, held her hand while looking from side to side.

"You run home, Maria," said another sister, looking so scared and different to the girl who had played hop, skip and jump with her a few hours earlier. "We have to work too. You run straight home and don't talk to any strangers."

But it didn't work like that in the Philippines. At the crossing near the UN building, a few blocks from home, a man in a suit came up to her with a charming smile. He looked like one of the handsome actors she had seen in a western movie, as nice as could be. An English gentleman, sober and kind.

"Where are you going, my little beauty?" he said, looking one way and then the next, like the other man, dragging hard on a cigarette.

Long-legged Maria was fifteen and strangely assured.

"I'm going home."

The man ruffled her hair and begged to differ. "Are you sure you want to do that now, my princess?"

"I think so."

"You don't want to come and play with me? Have some fun?"

"What kind of fun?" It was not a concept she was familiar with. "I don't want to have fun with you. You're too old to play."

"Don't be like that." The man slipped an arm round her shoulder. "I'll show you some new games."

"I don't think so." Maria slipped from under the man's arm and ran across the street in the blink of an eye, dodging a jeepney with 'Jesus loves you' emblazoned across the top of its windshield.

She stopped, looked back at the man and bellowed: "Eat shit and Die."

Then she set off at a run, whispering "oh my lord, forgive me" over and over again, and didn't stop until she got home.

The next time she visited Ermita, three years later, it was as a respectable Bunny Girl, where she served drinks to rich tourists at a five-star hotel with her bottom sticking out. She never had to service the Ermita low-lifers and never had to sleep with anyone, except a colonel in the army who was a regular and who once spectacularly let off a round in the lobby as he was checking his gun at the door. But he was soon posted to the south to fight a Muslim insurgency and nobody ever heard from him again.

Then came Wanchai and now, happiest of all, she was in the New Territories, where the customers were all regulars and no one, so far, had insisted on playing with her against her will.

I knew none of this at the time. Maria didn't know me, or anyone for that matter, well enough to share her story.

A FURTIVE TORMENT arrived at the Honest Bar wearing an Afro wig, a shawl and wrap-around sunglasses. He bumped into me in the dim light and said "whoops".

"Steady on, pal. Sorry, Chris, is that you?"

"Shhh."

Torment fumbled on to a stool, feeling his way with his hand along the bar.

"Stevie Wonder, right? I'm guessing."

"Why do you insist on living in the middle of nowhere? It took me hours to get here." Torment turned to ah-Fei. "Double gin and tonic, Captain."

"I like it here," I said.

"Of course you do. You're hopeless, Hadley."

I was ready to ignore that and was about to ask where he had picked up the "captain" thing when he turned and launched at me.

"Why are you trying to destroy me?" he said.

"That's the first time I've heard you use my first name, by the way. How am I trying to destroy you? Am I allowed to look at you? While we have our chat?"

"That stuff about my being a coward and a racist. Where did you get that from?"

"I didn't get it from anywhere. You want to ask that guy with the gun where he got it from."

"You didn't make it up?"

"Ha! That's rich. You think we can do that? Just make stuff up?" I could have sworn I had had this conversation not so long ago. "Of course I didn't make it up. He tried to kill you! I went to his cell and spoke to him in person. He said all that stuff. And more."

"I've been to see him too. I found myself apologizing to him and I don't even know what I've done wrong. He's one confused fucker." Chris stared at me as though expecting an explanation. I stared back as though wanting to rip the Afro wig off his head and stuff it down his throat. "And it seems he is of the opinion that he is a bit of a failure, because he didn't kill me. What really gets him is that he feels he has made his organisation a laughing stock. What do you think about that?"

"Don't make me laugh," I said. "Of course it's a laughing stock. I mean look at its bloody stupid name. What is it trying to do, anyway? Last I heard, the Daily Telegraph had found two Chinese families in Jaffna. They were in a tourist group from Beijing."

"Exactly."

"Exactly what?"

"That would be a good place to start. To find out what the group is trying to do, and why a man would be willing to kill someone famous, or himself, or go to jail for the rest of his life to help it do it. Isn't that what reporters do, find things out? What is this group trying to do?"

Don't you start, you toff. I leant closer. "I *have* tried to find out, along with a lot of people who know much more about Sri Lankan separatist groups than me. This is exactly what reporters do, but so far we have had no success. We have drawn a blank."

"Don't let me teach you your business, Hadley, but isn't there a story there in your drawing a blank? Perhaps there is no such Muslim separatist group."

"He isn't a Muslim separatist."

"I rest my case. Perhaps he's a put-up job. Did you stop to think of that? Perhaps it's a set-up. If so, you've swallowed it hook, line and sinker. Shrubs will love you for that. Cheers."

Torment downed his drink in one and majestically gestured to ah-Fei for another round. Ah-Fei, who had been monitoring this new man's movements, flinched when Torment's glass hit the table.

"You're a bit of a disgrace to your profession, I reckon. Who knows what nonsense you've been writing over the years? I'm surprised you haven't got hurt."

"I take my work very, very seriously. You can't say that about me."

"I can't say that you take your work very, very seriously. You're right. But I can say what I like about you. And I wanted to tell you that nothing you do can hurt me. The power of the press, if that is what you think it is, is nothing up against the kind of power I have behind me." I thought of Joe sitting in his grand house on the Peak. "I saw an old Bond film yesterday, 'Tomorrow Never Dies'," Torment said. "Nothing in it that wasn't done bigger and better in 'On Her Majesty's Secret Service' back in the sixties. The bad guy was about as menacing as a window cleaner. Should have called it 'Yesterday Once More'."

"That's a Carpenters song."

"I know."

"Oh."

"I would have done it all bigger and better. I get what I want, you see. No one pisses around with me. I can get you off this film by clicking my fingers. And you might as well be the first to know – I am going to be the next James Bond."

"No you're not."

"Oh yes I am."

"Oh no you're not. Who says?"

"I say. Because I am in earnest. And because I am in earnest, I will not fail. It's the power to do as one wishes, something you have obviously had no experience of. Like the power to bonk anyone I like. It's a fine thing. As an actor, that's the power I have. Anyone. Any time."

"Okay. Katherine Hepburn. Here. Right now."

"You don't get it. That's probably why you live out here in the middle of a swamp, away from all civilisation. Fortune favours the brave. And anyone who gets in my way should watch out."

Torment had never looked so malevolent.

"My sister hated you more than I did," I said, immediately regretting it. "More than I *do*."

"Your sister? What's she got to do with the price of a cup of tea?"

"Cup of tea?"

"Did I know your sister? Probably. O-M-G, I do believe something's coming back to me. Hardly a feather in my cap." At the mention of hat, he pulled off his Afro wig. "What do you think, anyway? Does the trick, what? Where's that tart behind the bar gone?"

I realised I wasn't protesting enough at the same moment that I realised that I was being deliberately provoked.

"Maria's not a tart," I said, resolving to go into action and put my head above the parapet. My neck tightened, my voice hardened and by the time I had said "tart", I was on my feet, had thrown what was left of my drink into Torment's face, and had begun a long flail with my right arm, the target Torment's chin, to the sound of scraping chairs.

The last time I had tried the flail (Diagram 1: The Flail), I had been drunk in the Tally Ho in Kentish Town many years earlier. I remembered the sensation. As soon as you strike the pose, i.e. clench the fist, cock the forearm, open the eyes terrifyingly wide and lean back ready to strike, you are seized with a vision of how you look, which of course is ridiculous. But there is no turning back. You realise that this is a half-cocked, half-baked imitation of Sean Connery and that in turn does nothing for your confidence in landing the blow. Once you begin the flail, two things are crystal clear: one, you should have reconsidered resorting to violence; and two, the flail itself will take a scenic route and the time between start and impact will be about a quarter of an hour. During the flail, your opponent will have stepped aside with a frown, made a pot of tea and settled down to a good book.

Working to my advantage was the fact that Torment had been distracted by having a whisky thrown in his face. He had stood up and was brushing himself down. My clenched fist only found Torment's elbow, but at least it made contact – I wanted to smile and congratulate myself, but I remembered to look angry. Torment, shocked, held his elbow and said:

"What was that in aid of?"

I was aware of Maria taking my arm and leading me to the bar where I sat and stared menacingly at Torment.

"John Travolta," she said. "My god."

CHAPTER EIGHT

I WOKE UP at midday, opened my eyes and tried to focus. I was looking at a large Pink Panther. Or rather a Pink Panther, handing from the ceiling, was looking at me. It spun full circle and looked at me again. I sat upright. Where was I? Whose house was this? What happened last night? The double bed was empty. Then something clicked – I was in Maria's flat. I lay back, putting my hands under my head. "Maria," I said to myself.

Then came the first wince. Torment had been with me in the Honest Bar. There had been some sort of argument. Then came a stronger wince that expanded key heart valves. There had been a fight. I had thrown a punch. My heart was beating faster now and the winces were coming more regularly. I remembered Torment brushing himself down and then holding his elbow and saying "What was that all about?" or some such and then Maria leading me to the bar. Torment had been driven away in a limo. Maybe more than one. I saw myself pissing against a wall. No, wait. I was pissing after the accelerating limos and shouting, and *then* pissing against a wall. Yikes. And then falling asleep at Maria's place, a Spanish-style villa with a blue roof a ten-minute drive away, after singing along loudly to Johnny Bristol's 'Hang on in There Baby' in the taxi. And then waking up and making love. With beautiful Maria. What a glorious memory. It was life-affirming counter-collywobbles.

The door opened. Maria was wearing a towel round her body and a towel round her head, carrying a cup of coffee and using

'Mr Tony's Book of Movies' as a tray.

"Maria?"

"Yes, Hadley. It's me."

She put down the book, took the towel from around her head and let the other towel, the really life-affirming towel around her body, fall to the ground. Good grief, it was a sight to behold. And everything was so fresh and wet. And I wasn't dreaming.

I took another taxi through the Lam Tsuen valley to my village feeling extraordinary. So this is happy. This is no longer glum man in bar. I wondered how my night had compared with Torment's. Or vice versa. I had asked Maria about Chris Torment's "power to bonk".

"If he had made a pass at you, what would you have done?"

"Shit, what do you think I am?"

"No. I mean on an ordinary night. If he had come on strong. I mean, is he right? About being a star? That he can get any woman he wants?"

"Piece of shit."

"I see."

Back at my flat, I opened the curtains and turned on the television and groaned. There was Torment *again*, splayed in a fat studio armchair, sounding off yet *again*. The man was just awful. A constant reminder of a life and supercilious people and small mindedness I thought I had left behind long ago.

"School was hard, no one can gainsay, but I also believe it built character. Like a rock. It was tough to make friends, but those friends you did make..."

"Stuck with you through thick and thin?" the presenter suggested.

"Stuck with you through thick and thin. Exactly."

I was holding my head and making high-pitched gnu noises. This man was one big flailing cliché. What was he talking about? What was he gainsaying?

"So let's get this straight. You were a boarder?" the presenter, a personable young Chinese American with a lisp, asked. "You lived on campus?"

"We were boarders, yes."

"Boys only."

"Indeed. In those days, most public schools were single sex. And I don't remember any hanky-panky after the lights went out."

"I'm sorry?"

"I mean it was a healthy environment and we all had girl-friends."

"Oh right."

I spread-eagled myself on the sofa. Memories of my sister, of Maria, of my flail, took turns to enliven me, to give my scotch-bloated heart a flutter, and to make me retch. And now Torment on the telly. "Too much air time! Too much air time! Please shut him up. Or ask him about his power, the power to bonk!"

"I'm sorry, Chris. Please continue. Let me just remind the audience at home, again, if you've just joined us, that we have the famous Ye Olde English Shakespearean actor Chris Torment in the studio today, and he's been telling us – is telling us – some anecdotes about his salad school days back in the U.K. Please go on."

The camera switched to Torment who was sweating hard.

"Ye Olde actor! Ye Olde actor!" I bellowed.

"Well, I'm not sure where I was," Torment said. "But I loved rugby and boxing. All character-building stuff."

"Why do you think there has been all this malicious gossip in the press? It seems pretty malicious. As if you could be a homosexual."

Where did this homosexual stuff coming from? What 'malicious gossip'? I was in the press business and it was news to me. Unless, unless... Unless this was Joe's Plan B.

"But don't get me wrong," Torment said. "There's nothing wrong with being homosexual. I mean I've got nothing against homosexuals. But I am now. I mean I am not."

"Not what?"

"I'm not homosexual. You mustn't believe all you read."

"Indeed," the presenter said, swishing back a quiff. "I read somewhere that you weren't homosexual."

"I rest my case."

"So I shouldn't believe it?"

Torment stared at the presenter. He hadn't a clue where he was in the conversation. So he laughed a flat "ha ha ha".

"Well, that was an incredible insight into Chris Torment's personality," the presenter said to camera. "It was like a real English tale with a kicker. The kind of tale, I reckon, that would ably support the kind of experience to benefit you in your later acting career, as Macbeth or Hamlet, perhaps?" Torment was frowning. "Or maybe the next James Bond, who knows? Did you see the new Bond film yet?"

"It was marvellous."

"And presumably you are next in line?"

Torment raised his hands in mock horror. "As far as I know, I am not up for the part."

"Go on, you can tell us."

"No, really. There have been no discussions along those lines."

"Go on, you can tell us."

"No, I can't. Of course..."

"You can tell us? Don't be a coward."

Torment managed to collect himself: "I was going to say, of course, that I presume you mean the part of James Bond."

"Oh yes," the presenter said, winding up the most uncomfortable interview ever televised in Hong Kong and turning again to the camera. Torment looked into the wings for support. "Ladies and gentlemen, do you believe that?" The tone of the question was "Do you believe that shit?" The presenter was pointing to Torment with his thumb. "Whether or not you do, of course, is up to you, but I'm willing to lay bets on who next picks up the

007 mantle with the associated licence to thrill. Chris Torment, thank you."

"Far too much air time," I said as the lights dimmed and the presenter leant forward to shake Torment's hand and banter until someone had turned off the camera.

"Got to get you out of my life, Chris," I said. "One way or the other."

WHILE CHRIST TORMENT was suddenly everywhere in Hong Kong, Joe had suddenly disappeared. Having Joe in sight was unpleasant, but manageable. Having Joe out of sight was, to be honest, a bit of a nightmare.

I went in search and took the tram up the Peak, setting off along Harlech Road, the noise of cicadas and other deafening insects in the new spring greenery to my left. I passed joggers and tourists and two boys shooting what appeared to be air guns. I stopped to read graffiti on the cement propping up the hill. There was nothing offensive, not in English anyway; just lots of declarations of boys loving girls and vice versa and one 'Joe was here', which didn't make me smile. I turned into the cutting where Joe's limo had turned. The quiet of Harlech Road turned to absolute silence as I walked towards what I now saw was called 'The Circle'. I peered into long gardens next to white stuccoed bungalows and passed the untended tennis court. A blond woman was loading boxes into the back of a car in the drive next door to Joe's apparently empty house.

I loitered a while and then approached.

"Hello there."

The woman looked up, pushing the hair from her eyes, and smiled. "Hi."

"I see your neighbour has moved."

"Joe? Yes."

I stared as I suffered a minor relapse of my wandering. Where was that journalistic instinct?

"You have a lot of boxes," I said. "Do you happen to know where he's moved to?"

"I don't. Are you a friend?"

"Yes. I seem to have lost touch."

A car was pulling up into Joe's drive and my first reaction was to duck and hide, but it wasn't Joe. The driver was a woman and no one I knew.

"Your guardian angel, right?"

What did she mean? What did she know? "That was part of it."

"I miss him. He was very colourful. Loads of fun. I'm surprised he left in such a hurry."

Loads of fun? Could this be the same man? "Why's that?"

"He liked Hong Kong. Said he could put down roots here and that his job had only just begun."

"But what did he do, do you know? What was his job?"

"I never knew anything about that. He was a bit of a mystery. He seemed to love his fancy-dress parties."

Fancy-dress parties? I examined the car pulling up next door. The driver was Asian with big hair, checking something in her lap.

"Fancy-dress parties? Joe?"

"I saw him in fancy dress a few times. It was always very late at night. Once it was a tight Chinese tunic, like a Mao suit but much nicer. A bit like Dr No, if you ever saw that movie. Other times it was a white dinner jacket and an eye-patch."

"Like Blofeld."

"Ooh, I can see a trend. And he'd carry that cat with the diamond necklace."

"A cat?"

"I hate cats. That bloody cat has scared off all my birds."

The Asian woman was getting out of the car. I had to speak to her.

"Look, this beautiful lady might be able to help," the neighbour said.

The woman from the car was approaching Joe's front door.

"Anything else?" I feigned a laugh. "Joe. What a crazy guy."

"Once I saw him wearing a billowing white toga," the neighbour said.

"Good God."

"Like a Roman senator. He was a bit out of character that time. I think he might have had a bit too much to drink."

The woman from the car was turning the key at Joe's front door. "Almost certifiable, I reckon. Many thanks for that. I'll go and see if this lady knows anything."

I ran across the lawn and caught the woman as she was entering.

"Hi there."

"Hello."

I breathed in an expensive scent and took in the wide smile. Big round eyes on an oval face, eyebrows arched, hair done up in a bun with a dangerous silver skewer holding it in place. I guessed Korean.

"Boy," I said.

"Boy?"

"No. No boy. Sorry."

I was having a moment I supposed only men would understand. I wanted this woman immediately. There and then. Pull yourself *together*.

"Joe," I said. "My friend Joe used to live here."

"Yes?" The eyebrows were raised, the smile was innocent and affectionate. Smoothly applied lipstick, maybe a touch too much Max Factor No 5. Definitely Korean.

"I seem to have lost touch."

The woman looked across at the neighbour packing the boxes.

"What to do?" she said. "He didn't tell me where he was going, I am afraid. I am here to check the appliances."

"Well, can I come in? We were at a party here the other night and my friend..." I turned and waved at the neighbour who waved back. "...my friend thinks she may have left a ring in the bathroom."

"I'm afraid I am not allowed..."

"No, you don't have to worry. We've been here many times. It's the bathroom behind the drinks cabinet. Where Joe stocks his malt whisky. We're frequent visitors. What's your name?"

"I am Miss Kim."

"I'm Hadley." We shook and I held on to her hand a second too long. An old trick. "You are very beautiful, Miss Kim."

Miss Kim looked demurely at her feet then raised her head to meet my gaze.

"You're way out of your league, sleaze ball," she said.

I stepped back. "Well that's not very nice."

"Neither are you, jerk off. Just piss off. Or I'll tell your 'friend'."

"Look, I'm sorry if I've offended you, but..."

Miss Kim stepped into the house and slammed the door in my face. Way out of my league? Hel-lo? Have you ever *seen* Maria? I was furious. The neighbour was still at her car and watching. I waved and set off round the back of the house, keeping low so pasty-faced Miss Korea wouldn't see me through the windows. She had that spear in her hair after all.

But I didn't know what I was looking for. I didn't know what I was doing. My life was a game show with a particularly strange host who, depending on how the mood took him, appeared in a toga or a Mao suit. I opened the door to an outhouse where there were two rubbish bins. One was empty, the other about a quarter full of papers and magazines. I no longer cared about the dagger woman and turned the can noisily on its head and threw it aside. No messy food, just papers: advertising fliers, air miles offers, utility bills and magazines. I uncrumpled an envelope which looked like personal mail. It was a letter to Joe Stein, but the address on the front was different. It was a flat in Jaffe Road, a street full of cheap basement clubs and whore houses near Lockhart Road, the main bar street in Wanchai. Did Joe have an office there? Or an apartment? 30D Rich Mansion, Jaffe Road. I committed the address to memory.

CHAPTER NINE

WHEN I JOINED Shrubs and found I would have to travel to places unknown in times of trouble, I was given a piece of advice by a senior hack, a former Beijing bureau chief who echoed exactly what Joe had said more recently: write what you see. On drives into turbulent capitals when you don't know who is shooting at what, write what you see. Write about the two old women sitting in a window, staring at the sky, one of them clutching a doll. Write about the man with a shirt over his head running into an abandoned post office. Write about the two dogs bonking on a pedestrian crossing. They are all part of the big picture.

Baxter gave me the same advice now, after briefing me on my trip to Jaffna, in north Sri Lanka, where the flower-power stringer was still missing. And then a three-day trip with Torment to Macho Island.

A couple of days before departure, Adolf Lee threw a junk party to which all the 'I Love Hong Kong' cast and crew were invited, plus a few hangers-on, including the glum man in bar. Baxter was invited but he declined, instead offering his place to Fagin, the world's most anti-social sub-editor. Fagin hated junks and all their expat associations and he hated parties. Naturally, he also declined.

The junk set sail. I helped myself to the Black Label and leant with my back to the rail as I assessed the situation. There were lots of beautiful women onboard and I watched them as they talked and smoked. A Macau hydrofoil whistled past on the starboard side, leaving a trail in the water half a mile long. On the other side, a Discovery Bay ferry was about to cut across the junk's path. The lights of Hong Kong island rose up on the left, layers of skyscrapers gliding like plates across layers of lights behind. My brother, on seeing Hong Kong for the first time, had described it as a science fiction city. He imagined cartoon traffic of rocket taxis and shuttle buses nipping in and out of the buildings.

Two bald Chinese men came over and stood near me. I had briefly seen them with Panda Koo earlier and assumed they were bodyguards, though at the time my eyes were mostly on Panda's jeans. The men nodded at me but said nothing. Adolf Lee was surrounded and unapproachable. I had managed to catch the eye of both Gretel the audition woman and Candy Kam but neither showed any sign of recognition. Panda Koo looked so angry that I couldn't understand how anyone would dare try to talk to her. Never mind. I was enjoying the breeze, the booze and the bright lights.

Then I spotted Torment. He was on the far side of the boat with that prick of an actor who played Magnus, looking earnest. Seconds later, Maria appeared at the top of the stairs, brushing down a ridiculously short black skirt. She skipped over to Torment who slipped his hand around her back and introduced her to Magnus. My heart skipped a couple of beats. I suffered an overwhelming pang of jealousy, the likes of which I hadn't known since I was a teenager.

"First your sister, now pretty Maria," whispered Joe, who had appeared from nowhere. I smelt an expensive aftershave.

"She wouldn't," I said. "What makes you say that?"

"He's shameless."

"But she's not."

"Whatever you say."

And then Maria caught my eye and beamed and rushed across the deck, her hips doing their best to rock the boat from stern to hull. "Hadley! Chris said you would be here."

"Maria. You're beautiful."

"Oh stop it."

My heart was racing. Maria had a protruding ridge down the middle of her upper lip which flattened and disappeared when she smiled. Her eyes were milky and bright.

"You're here with Chris," I said. Really observant.

"He's bar-fined me for the night. Huge."

"Wonderful."

"But I told him, no jiggy-jiggy."

"Oh, good." I inhaled another exotic and expensive scent.

"I only do jiggy-jiggy with people I like."

I exhaled an "oh Maria" which almost came out as "Ave Maria" and had a life of its own, cracking on the second syllable of her name. It came from nowhere and took me by surprise. It also prompted Maria to raise her hand to my face, with a frown, and then to pull it away, a gesture Torment caught in a brief glimpse over his shoulder.

"I have to go back to him," she said. "He wants me by his side."

"Of course," I said.

The power to bonk anyone, any time, Torment had said. Maria squeezed my hand and tripped back to Torment, who greeted her with a big, phony "ah, there you are" look and pretended I did not exist.

I turned to the drinks table and accepted a scotch with a shaking hand. This feeling I had with Maria was completely new. It was a powerful, alien force. Was it possible, god forbid, that I was having a heart attack?

Near me an old American with shaggy black hair and a cigar was speaking to a group of assorted aides. Everyone was wearing far too much jewellery in and around their nostrils and mouths. I listened.

"... I still think making a film is a bit like creating the universe.

Except without the day of rest. What you must tell me is which is worse, the fact that I once thought film making was like creating the universe, or that I still think it?"

I wanted to vomit all over the man's unkempt hair, but managed to keep myself in check. I caught sight of Maria, now apparently alone. I also caught sight of Joe standing by the wheel house, staring at me and nodding towards Maria. I walked to the railing to the right of a couple of fat skinheads with earrings and headrings and cranium scars. Closest to me was a man whose jeans were hung below his hips and about to drop. Written on the back of his t-shirt was 'Bog Man'. Joe had talked about Bog Man, who was a cinematographer at the top of his field. He belonged in a field.

"...In the lights on the water I see a thousand shards of an oriental night," Bog Man was saying. "I see your love skipping like a water lily over my dead body..."

What was the matter with these film people? All that creativity and imagination running wild and turning them into people who could barely speak a sentence without making the average casual listener, a resident of the real world, want to throw up all over them. In one way or another, they were all bog men.

Adolf Lee approached with two men in suits and I was beginning to look forward to the junk turning around and steaming back to Central.

"Hadley, forgive me for interrupting. These two gentlemen are from Belgium. They are commodities dealers and I thought you'd have a lot to discuss." Adolf Lee looked at the two and added: "He's a journalist."

I knew as much about commodities dealing as I did about the greater Brussels sewage system. The two men were identical. They looked like Mormon missionaries, without the sense of mischief.

"Hi there," I ventured. "So you subscribe to the Shrubs news service?"

"You work for them?"

"*Mais oui.*"

"Commodities?" the one on the left said.

"General political news. Some economic news. Some commodities, yes. Metals, grains and the like."

The two shuffled their feet. "If you come into our office, you can tell we are commodity traders," the one on the right said.

"Oh? How's that? I cannot tell that you are Belgian, by the way. Your accents are perfect."

"Thank you," the one on the left said. "Our telephones."

"Sorry?"

"Our telephones will tell you that we are commodity traders," the one on the right said. "They're green and yellow and shaped like corn on the cob."

Silence. Not a hint of irony or self-deprecation. They were waiting for a reaction. I coughed. "Your telephones are shaped like corn on the cob? That'll certainly have people guessing." Corn on the cobblers. "What's your connection with the movie, if you don't mind my asking?"

"We helped raise funds. Matched up a couple of investment opportunities."

"Commodities?"

"*Pas du tout.* Norwegian bond market. We introduced a hedging tool."

"A hedging tool? Like a Black & Decker?"

I desperately tried to think of a commodities-related joke that would have them rolling in the aisles. *Roulant dans les allées.* The one on the left frowned and then let loose like the nervous beginning to an audition for a movie extra.

"Got to short the Hong Kong dollar," he said. "They've got to raise interest rates or revalue the yuan. Either way you've got a head-and-shoulders straddle which will extrapolate the long bond and raise the benchmark puts. Then, once property prices hit bottom, no one will be able to pay their mortgages and red chips and H shares will hit the fan and you can call your Oslo option."

"Forward," his friend added.

"Right. You can call your option forward."

This is an impressionist version of the conversation, you understand. As I didn't understand one word of what they were saying, it is impossible to repeat word for word. I do remember that I considered the option of jumping over the railing into the path of a fast approaching Macau hydrofoil. I would have been less out of my depth. "I can call it forward?"

"What choice would you have? I reckon put in a million now and you'll have 100 times that in two weeks. You've got to short the Hong Kong dollar. Then, and only then, I would seriously consider Norwegian equities."

"But what if, before I took the Norway route, I bucked the trend and did a 180-degree turn?"

"Don't quite follow you, I'm sorry."

"Well, what if I did as you advised, and called my Oslo option and told him to get his skates on (ha ha). But what if then, instead of calling it forward, which presumably the whole market would be doing by this stage, what if I called it... backward? Then I could really think about the whole Norway package."

The dealers were staring at me with their arms folded. The one on the right pulled out a phone and punched in some numbers.

"You think you're a pretty funny guy, right?" he said while waiting for someone to answer.

"I like to think I have my moments." I wanted to catch Maria's eye.

"No, it's that British sense of humour. It's great. Standing on the sidelines of life and mocking everything you see. Most people have it broken out of them by the time they're eighteen."

He turned his back and walked away, talking into the phone. His friend shrugged his shoulders, patted me on the cheek, and said: "Touched."

The stroke of midnight two nights later found me in one of the packed Wanchai basement clubs, where the girls were all Filipina pros and the Filipino band played awful Deep Purple songs. I remembered Joe's Jaffe Road address and the opening chords of 'Smoke on the Water' convinced me that now was the time to investigate.

Rich Mansion is an ancient apartment block shaped like a disposable lighter, thin and high. There was an old man asleep at the reception desk. I had no plan, but wondered if a bit of authority would help. My nodding acquaintance in Wanchai, the British detective, would be perfect for the job (I was even pretty sure where to find him at this time of night). But I pressed on alone. A slow, rickety lift arrived to take me to the top floor. Joe's address was 30D. I had the sense to get out of the lift two floors below and then quietly climb up the fire stairs to, and then past, Joe's floor, briefly looking through a panel of meshed glass on my way up to the roof. An upside-down Chinese good luck sign was on the door of 30B; an incense offering with two tangerines sat next to the mat. A sign on the door of 30C said 'do not enter when light is red', but there wasn't any light. *Du-uh*. I reckoned 30D was on the northeast of the building, overlooking Jaffe Road. I reached the roof one floor above, expecting some kind of view, but there was precious little, Rich Mansion surrounded on all sides by ever taller and richer mansions. There was the glare of neon from Lockhart Road below, the click-clack of mahjong tiles, the cries of a couple of babies, the rushing sound of gas burners from restaurants at street level, and the inevitable smell of fried tofu. I leant over the newly painted side of the building where I supposed Joe's flat to be. Bingo. The lights were on. Did that mean Joe was in there? What difference did that make? I could just go and knock on the door and say hello. But then what? I had a strange feeling; those collywobbles were returning. There was some sort of resolution in store. What I needed was a mirror.

Back at ground level, in a bar a few yards to the south, I tried to explain to a twenty-one-year-old dancer called Suzie why I needed to borrow her compact.

"It will only be for an hour or so. I'll bring it back, I promise."

"But why do you need it?"

"I want to lean over the roof of a building and spy on an old man with a ponytail in his flat."

"You always make jokes, Hadley. Tell me why you want it."

Oh boy. "I'll tell you what. I'll bar-fine your compact."

"What?"

"I'll pay you for your compact. How about $50 for an hour."

"You don't bar-fine me, but you want to bar-fine my makeup? You one crazy English fucker."

"Well, what do you say? I'll also need a coat hanger."

Ten minutes later, the guard was still asleep and I made it back to the roof of Rich Mansion. I wound the end of the unravelled coat hanger round the open compact and held it up to see if would stay put and at the right angle. The compact stayed put, but the stuff inside, the powdery, flesh-coloured cake stuff, tumbled in one chunk on to my face.

"For fuck's *sake*."

It was in my eyes, my mouth, my hair and up my nose. Why do women use this... gunk? I spat and swore again and set to work. I leant over the concrete wall. The lights were still on. I lowered my device until I could see into the room (the curtains were open, or the blind was up), and what I saw as I tweaked the mirror from side to side made me gasp.

The room was empty. Completely empty. White walls, parquet floor, and nothing else. And yet the light was on. Why? I raised the mirror and stood back. The whitewash off the wall had left a foot-wide stripe of chalk or dry paint across my jacket. I walked to the front of the building and looked over. The lights were on in a different room. A man was arguing with the driver of a red taxi on the street below. I lowered my contraption again, careful not to let it go too far and not to bang it against the glass.

I saw Maria sitting at a round melamine table, her hair done back in a ponytail. The shake in my hand was amplified by the length of the coat hanger and it was difficult to get a focus. Maria was looking across the table, as though being spoken to by someone out of sight, her head dipped, her eyes looking up through her lashes. The look on her face was that of adventure, satisfaction. Of relaxation. I stood up, catching my jacket on a newly painted red lightning rod. I didn't want to have another look in the room, but I had to find out what was going on. I had never seen Maria wear her hair like that.

I moved along the roof top to try to get a narrower angle into the room, to see who else was there. I lowered the bar-fined compact (which had proved to be a real bargain at $50, the price of a regular beer at the Rawhide) but could see nothing except a Chinese landscape print on the wall. I slowly raised the mirror, moved back to my original position and gently lowered it again.

Maria was laughing as Torment, who was now sitting next to her at the table looking lascivious and lizard-like, placed his hand on her leg. My periscope gave a hard, involuntary 'clack' against the glass.

"Bugger."

I saw Maria react in the mirror in the split second before I lifted it away from the window. A guilty freeze frame. I caught my jacket again on the lightning rod and this time Suzie's compact went flying, bouncing off laundry poles about four floors down and curling away into the street.

I thought fast. Should I go down and confront them before they came up? Would they come up to investigate? If so, how long would it take them to come up? Would I have time to get below their level on the fire stairs before they started coming up? If they came up and saw me, covered in white chalk, red paint and pink gunk, what would they do? What would I do? Starting to panic, I ran to the back of the building and looked over. About three feet down was the roof covering the fire-escape stairs leading from one of Joe's doors or windows. There was a low rail around the edge, making it an unlikely balcony, but a safe place to hide.

A door went bang not far away. I climbed over the wall. What was that line about not raising your head above the parapet? I eased myself down on to the ledge, my face to the wall. Another door banged and I held my breath.

"I saw something flash pink," I heard Maria say. No response from anyone. "And then it went away. But it hit the window."

"Some asshole," another woman said. "Some *jerk off*. Come on, Maria, forget it."

Some jerk off. Now pangs of jealousy tore through me like a silver dagger through a Korean big-hair bun. Was it jealousy? Or was it just a pure *thrill*? I had the hots for *both* of them. But hold your horses! Where did Torment fit in? Or Joe? Were they both bonking both of them? Worse than that, was Joe *filming* them? I felt a little overwhelmed as I pondered these permissive permutations, crouched on the roof of a thirtieth-floor fire-escape with a frown breaking through the Max Factor. My heart was beating so hard it was no longer safe to stay. My heart was rocking my whole frame. I straightened up, half expecting to see the three of them waiting for me. No one was there.

Back at street level, I retrieved the compact which by the look of it had been run over about forty times. Inside there was an inscription: *To our darling Suzie on her graduation, from her proud and loving parents.*

Sorry, Suzie.

CHAPTER TEN

TWO DAYS LATER I was sitting in the economy section of a Sri Lanka North Air Airbus. The slogan was 'The Sky's the Limit for Sri Lanka North Air', which I found disturbing. If the sky were the limit (subjunctive!), how on earth would they land? And if something's the limit, it usually means you are angry with it. So the Sri Lanka North Air pilots are angry with the sky? That's no way to fly. Torment's camera crew and aides were in business class and Torment, naturally, was up in first. Crammed in at front of economy, I caught a glimpse of Torment coming back to josh with his team and pat a passing air stewardess on the bottom. Write what you see, I thought. A malevolent ponce, as fake as a game show host, turning on the charm and insinuating himself into yet more nice people's lives.

I fell asleep and dreamt that Adolf Lee had appeared at the front door of Joe's house and insisted on being allowed in. "I rule the world, as a director. I rule everyone," he said as he unbuckled his sword and sat down in a bowl of hot water.

"The difference is, at the end of the day, when the cameras stop rolling, I rule nobody. I am another face in the crowd. Whereas Torment..."

"Yes?"

"Torment rakes people. He's a charming rake. He rakes people like I rake leaves. I put my leaves on the compost heap, in Norfolk. Up against the wall. Of the Old Rectory."

"What are you talking about?"

I was woken sharply by a stewardess tugging at my sleeve.

"Sir?"

"Yes? Sorry, I was asleep."

"That's okay, sir. Need your head sex."

"Need what?"

"Head sex. Before we land."

I assumed I was still dreaming and looked around. I was confused and concerned. I checked my watch. "Do we have enough time?"

The girl reached across and grabbed my head set and took off down the aisle.

"Are you Chinese?" I called after her, half-heartedly.

Torment was to meet the prime minister and try to look serious as he discussed international aid. The east coast of Jaffna had been ravaged by the storm, but Macho had been saved by some geological freak of Nature. My job was to track down the whisky priest, presumably still in Jaffna, and to get to the Chinese homeland. I had done some homework. From my Sri Lankan guidebook, I found that Macho was actually a sprawling, lush archipelago which had been runner-up to Thailand in the choice for the location of 'The Man with the Golden Gun'. It had one of the most corrupt local governments on earth and had been colonised by every country in the world at one time or other – except for Canada. Poverty and violence were entrenched, the book said, "but with a little thoughtful planning and plenty of sun block, there is no reason to let this spoil your holiday".

Jaffna was dry and ruined, nearly three decades of war having smashed the place to smithereens. What hadn't been destroyed was strewn with landmines, some of them pretty, bright-coloured bomblets, designed to be picked up by children. Many had a delayed response, so the children would take them home, play with them for a couple of days, and then the explosion would take out a whole family.

I found the stringer's office down a tiny street between a tailor's and – progress! – a Chinese takeaway. Out in the open, old men in sarongs sat sweating at ancient typewriters, making a living adding to the mind-numbing bureaucracy by writing pedantic letters for people looking for government jobs or seeking compensation for their ruined homes. I climbed four flights of stairs with no lights and walked through a door with Shrubs written twelve inches high in drawing pins. The five people inside, half of them sifting through cardboard boxes on the floor, stopped what they were doing and stared balefully at me. One man with a paunch got up and with a small bow, introduced himself as Leon, the office manager.

"We are beholden," Leon said. "That you travel through the war zone to greet us is an honour."

"I am afraid you have taken me by surprise." I had assumed that Waverly, like most stringers, worked alone. "I didn't know we had a manager. Where's Waverly?"

Leon bowed again. "Is it that you don't like me, sir?"

"Excuse me?"

"Don't you like me? Of an evening?"

I walked through to the priest's office. A wizened old man was brushing the carpet, raising huge clouds of dust. Waverly's desk was littered with cuttings and press releases. On the top of his spike was a carbon duplicate of an old-fashioned telegram dated a day earlier.

"Jaffna is a poisonous town and I think I've got dysentery stop Everyone I meet is plotting something and the hostility has been too depressing for words stop Adios stop."

"He is gone into the air." The office manager was at the door. He had changed his shirt and reinforced his deodorant.

"Look," I said. "Who writes telegrams in this day and age? I don't know who you are or what you are doing. But my job is to find out."

"Please do not be angry, sire. I do my work, as Mr Waverly has instructed all these years. Do you like my colourful shirt?"

I changed tack. "Has anyone been to the Chinese takeaway next door?"

Leon looked puzzled. "For one's eating pleasure?"

"Yes, and no."

"You are hungry for one?"

"For one what? Do you have any information on the Chinese?"

"Wait." Leon skipped out of the office to a back room and came back and handed over a menu. "Luckily for you."

"I am going to interview them." I spoke as though issuing a threat, curling up the menu and pointing it at Leon. "And then I am going to find Waverly. Excuse me."

"Ask them about number twenty-two," Leon called after me. "Ask them where they find the balls to make such a recipe."

I ran downstairs and into the takeaway shop, where the door gave a familiar Sotobech high street ring as it opened. But there was no one inside. There was a half-finished bowl of noodles on the Formica counter and an out-of-date calendar on the wall next to some Lunar New Year greetings in red and gold. A tassel curtain hung over a doorway to the back.

"Anybody at home?" I made my way to the foot of some stairs and started up. "Hello?"

At the top, a door stood ajar and an old Chinese man was sitting on a bed, watching television. He wore a pair of shorts and no top and had a can of beer in his hand. "Hello?" I said softly. "I'm sorry if I'm disturbing you."

"Not at all. You've come with the boxes?"

"Boxes?"

"Boxes. Yes. From Hong Kong."

"No. I'm afraid not. I've come to ask about the DALJC," I said, breaking all the rules about interviewing someone you don't know on an emotive subject. You don't just jump in with two feet.

What the man did next was surprising, largely because of the agility with which he did it – he jumped up with two feet, turned off the television and leant against the wall as relaxed as could be. Something was wrong.

"It would only take a few minutes," I added. "I work for Shrubs News Agency which has an office upstairs. I have come here with Chris Torment and I was wondering if you knew anything about the Democratic Association..."

"I know nothing about such a group," the old man said. "I'm just here waiting for my boxes."

Time to calm things down. "Well, is there any chance of getting something to eat?"

"Something to eat?"

"Yes. Something to eat. From your restaurant."

The man looked at his watch. "It's one o'clock."

"I was thinking of having some lunch."

"Well, we could give it a shot." The man walked to the door. "Ming-min!" he called down the stairs. He went back to his bed. "Go down now, sir. Ming-min will serve you. Before you go..."

"Yes?"

"You said you were here with Chris Torment."

"Yes."

He sat down carefully, as though in pain. "Chris Torment's a nob."

Downstairs again, I glanced at the menu, which dramatically claimed to have 'the finest speciality'. The tassel curtain moved and a Chinese girl, about nineteen, with a flower in her hair and out of breath, came through. She was startlingly beautiful. She looked like of one of the girls in the 1930s Shanghai cigarette ads.

"Well, hello." I leant on the counter towards her breasts. "You must be Ming-min. Never in a million years did I expect to find such a lotus blossom as you hiding in this godforsaken place. Why on earth you Chinese would like to make a homeland..."

"Did Mr Waverly send you?" Ming-min said, playing with a nail on her manicured hands. She was looking at the door behind me.

I looked at her. Her shoulders held back, head held high. The posture was perfect.

"Waverly, my little jasmine flower?" I looked at the blossom in her hair. "What do you know about Mr Waverly?"

Ming-min reached up and pressed her slim fingers against my mouth.

"He wears a codpiece," she said. I detected a Hartlepool accent. "He's a scumbag, but I can't talk of such things now."

Ming-min swept around the front of the counter and took me by the arm. "Go now. I will see you soon," she said. "Once the boxes have arrived."

She pushed me out into the street and closed the door with a tinkle, turning the 'open' sign to 'closed'. She dashed back behind the curtain. Barking mad, I thought. What a waste – but hardly surprising in such a dump. I looked round the back of the building, but could not find another entrance. I gave up and left to find Waverly.

The priest's home was a suite at a waterfront hotel with teak floors and a sea spray and a month of dirty laundry tucked under the bed. I was going through the drawers when the phone went. It was my news editor.

"So where's the flower-pot priest?" Baxter asked.

"Haven't been able to trace him yet. Did you know he has an office with five people in it?"

"Oh no! Not an office with people in it?"

"I mean he's a stringer. Yet he's got an office with Shrubs written on the door. I met a Chinese girl, a new contact, who knows him intimately. She's a close friend. An informative and reliable source. You got my telegram? I didn't know you could send telegrams in this day and age."

"Never mind him now. Where's Torment? Actually, never mind him now either. I've got a great BBC story here which we need to match. Just five or six paragraphs. I'm emailing it now."

"What's happened?"

"An onion boat's dumped its load at sea."

"You'll have to speak up. I thought you said an onion boat's dumped its load at sea."

"Great story. It's also budget day in Sri Lanka."

"Budget day?"

"Let's not worry about that. Give me the onions."

An Australian ship unable to dock because of some security breach had dumped its load of red onions off Macho. The captain had decided to cut his losses and look for trade elsewhere. The onions had washed up along the beaches and the locals were picking them up and selling them at roadside stalls. I found the names of a couple of nearby hotels and rang the managers. It seemed the BBC story was spot on. I emailed back six paragraphs thinking life was too short.

"Overweight white tourists flocking to tropical Macho's golden beaches are turning red in the sun and peeling. So are the onions."

Five hours later, Torment and I were strapped into our seats in an ancient Avro transport plane and were sweating as it began its descent into Macho itself.

"This had better be quick," Torment said. "I've got a career to be getting on with."

I thought of the DALJC press releases which had been delivered to my hotel room in little square buff envelopes, written by typewriter, with red showing on top of some letters from the dual red and black ribbon. The English was pompous, not unusual for Sri Lanka. Words like 'modalities' and 'siblings' and 'thrice' were commonplace. So was 'commonplace'. There was an emblem at the top of each sheet which appeared to have been made with a rubber stamp and featured the Great Wall. The Great Wall of Macho.

"Sir Christopher Torment shall die a thrice-fold death of modalities unknown should he set forth in the glorious Chinese homeland of Macho," said one.

"The Democratic Association for the Liberation of Jaffna Chinese and her siblings across the Chinese-speaking world speak not once, not twice, but thrice for the liberation of Jaffna Chinese," said another. *"And if Torment should arrive, he will be dispatched."*

I had tried to corroborate the letters, which only seemed to be sent to me. If other newspapers or agencies were getting them, they were ignoring them. A Sri Lankan police officer told one of Waverly's mates DALJC was probably a front for some other, bigger and more dangerous group. Well, there you go then.

The plane was dropping fast. I had been told what to expect – the last ten minutes of the approach had to be flown just a few feet from the water. It was something to do with heat diffusion; fly that low and the surface-to-air missiles can't get a lock, not that anyone had ever heard of a missile being fired from Macho. I was convinced the plane was going to ditch. It was going too slowly, the pilot couldn't seem to keep the thing on an even keel. The wings seemed to be clipping the waves, first one side and then the other. If a wing clipped the water, that would be it. I imagined the impact and the horizontal cartwheel of the plane. I saw a few small fishing boats. Missiles can't be fired from fishing boats, someone had said. They are fired from land. So the nearer we get to the island, the more likely we are to be shot down.

"Did you see the pilot?" Torment shouted above the rattle and din of the engine roaring outside about three feet from my ear.

"What?"

"Did you see the pilot?"

Torment was sitting in the aisle seat, gripping the arm rests tightly. His knuckles shone like vanilla ice-cream. No, I didn't see the pilot, but I saw you and Maria through that Wanchai window, you bastard.

"I saw him before we took off," Torment said. "I talked to him. He's from the Ukraine. I think we'll be okay."

"What do you mean?"

"I looked in his shopping bag. Only saw one bottle of vodka."

There was a sudden, high-pitched scream from the engines and the plane lifted sharply. I saw a narrow strip of beach and at the same time realised that Torment had just shared a joke. The plane skimmed the top of a line of palm trees and then dropped again, skipping over mud huts and brush. There was a volcano in the distance. I turned round and caught the eye of two Sri Lankan media ministry officials three rows back. Both grinned back malevolently. This is a man's world, their faces were saying. You don't belong here.

The Avro was flying over barbed wire and bunkers now. I reminded myself to write down 'barbed wire and bunkers' in my notebook. Every other palm tree was missing its fronds. The plane slapped down hard on the tarmac. Torment gave an involuntary clap and I joined in. The engines roared and there was a hissing and a shrill needle of a noise which appeared to be coming from my headrest. There were also some derisory noises from behind after the clapping had died down.

The press bus sped into downtown Macho sandwiched between a motorcade of army security in front and behind, motorcyclists riding shotgun. They hurtled down a narrow road, fearful of sniper attacks and landmines. I jotted down what I could see: Brazilian and New Zealand architecture with holes in the walls; some houses in perfect condition set back from the road with verandas and dogs lying in the shade; more palm trees with their heads shot off, looking like pencils stuck in the ground; a health club, a computer school, a shop selling nothing but rubber hoses; a Japanese-style house marked 'Top Judge's Residence'... I had a brief relapse. I thought about my sister, Pamela. I had to ask her about Torment. I hadn't seen Pamela in more than fifteen years but knew she lived in Scotland and had three kids and was separated from a husband whose beet farm in the Fens had gone bankrupt. Did Scotland ever rule Macho? Did the Fens? Now we were at another air base, surrounded by commandos. The press were being escorted fast across a dusty airstrip to another plane.

What's it all about, Alfie? A portly brigadier pulled me aside, taking my travel bag and pinning me against a flaky wall.

"Good fellow, Mr Hadley. We have had an urgent call from your office, via military headquarters, one in a million, as the lines of communication are invariably affected by the troubles. Thrice already today."

I watched the man's lips move under his huge moustache. They were puckering. This was a men-only tropical paradise where girls did not get a look in. It was all khaki uniforms, pot stomachs and puckering parades. Puck off, the load of you.

"Sorry?"

"The message is that we must take good care of you and the honourable stage and screen actor, Sir Christopher Torment. Before we take you to the monsoon beaches. A bit of R&R."

"Thanks very much, Brigadier. He's not a sir by the way."

"I see him in the distance. What a fine figure of a man. I understand that you, personally, were particularly brave in foiling an assassination attempt."

"It was nothing. Anyone would have done the same."

"I think not. The fellow is an English arse. And now he is beholden to our care. For we are to take you to a particular locale where you also may find some local Chinamen."

"Chinamen?"

"Alas, yes. Though I am not yet officially apprised of their presence." Apprised of their presence? Say what? "None of us, officially, if truth be told, has been apprised of any Chinese terrorist presence."

"You mean the DALJC?"

The brigadier shrugged his shoulders. "It is a Chinese puzzle you find in the newspapers," he said. "Like the crossword puzzles."

This time it was a helicopter that was to fly us away, a huge, loud, spartan machine carrying nothing that wasn't black metal or canvas, inscriptions and instructions and first aid warnings in Cyrillic. Torment, the brigadier, a couple of captains and I ran to board at a crouch to keep some sort of buoyancy under the propellers and to keep the dust and stones that stung like bullets out of the face. I looked back. All the other journos were looking at us and complaining. Where's he going? Why aren't we going with him? One man was throwing up against some barbed wire.

The helicopter lunged away, vaguely stable, two gunners each side keeping a focused look-out for guerrillas below. The land was suddenly green and lush, heavy with forest. Men were throwing out nets from small boats on glistening rivers. I was perched on some metal and sacking, my hands gripping canvas straps so hard I thought I was going to get cramp. One of the gunners turned and caught my eye. The soldier winked and gave a reassuring smile. He couldn't have been more than twenty.

The helicopter skipped low over some magical lagoons, the gunners firing off a few rounds into the bush scattering flocks of pelicans, and then flew down a long, deserted beach, firing rounds and flares at the sea. We landed next to an empty swimming pool. This was the Lagoon Beach Hotel, on the northeast coast of Macho, once a happy resort for vacationing westerners, where expat American families would spend Christmas and New Year cheek by jowl with fat German paedophiles. Now it stood slap bang in a war zone. It was open, but empty, except at weekends when some Red Cross people would come and swim and eat barbecued shrimp and lie on the beach and read John le Carre novels. A team of old ladies still swept the red flagstones each morning and a waiter was on hand in the outside restaurant. But the thatched 'Disco Groove Nite Hut' on the beach had long since been abandoned and the pool was empty, except for some sand in the deep end and some crabs under the slide. The only nightlife was the mosquitoes, the only lights the fishing boats on the horizon. The drive from the hotel to the main road had to be cleared every morning. That meant soldiers walking slowly about a hundred yards into the bush either side, firing at random, and clearing the bush of any guerrillas. All roads had the same treatment. So did the beach. Occasionally a nervous soldier, hearing a noise, would turn and shoot a swollen-arsed monkey. Like Robert Redford with the snake in 'Butch Cassidy'.

"You will stay here two nights for such a hotel is convenient and commonplace for incognito assignments," the brigadier said. "But you must understand that we cannot guarantee your safety if you meet with these people. It is a *prima facie* case of your going it alone. With the bard."

"Thank you, Brigadier."

"And now it behoves me only to say good bye and to leave you. And to give you this."

The brigadier handed over a letter which I ripped open.

"Have to move things along," it said. "Stay where you are." It was signed Joe.

The brigadier gave a short bow and shook my hand.

"Good luck, Mr Hadley," he said. "Remember. He who dares wins."

The helicopter took off, scattering the crabs and remaining pool-side furniture, with the brigadier and the gunners grinning and waving out the side.

CHAPTER ELEVEN

TORMENT AND I ate fried fish by candlelight under the palms and demolished five large bottles of Three Fountains beer. I still hadn't broached the subject of Maria, but then neither had Torment, which was a bit of a worry. If anything had happened, he would have thrown it in my face. Or would he? Maybe Torment had fallen for her, just as I had.

"Anyone seeing us now would think we were a couple of poofs," Torment said.

I smiled. Another joke. Bit controversial, too. Stay where you are, Joe had said.

"Wouldn't do my career any good at all," he said. "What are we doing here, anyway?"

"The army said we should stay here, a bit of R&R, before they take us to the monsoon beaches. They've been in touch with my office. I don't know where the other press have gone."

"I don't see any monsoon damage here."

I looked at him. "No. There is no damage *here*. The army will take us to the damaged areas after we have relaxed for a bit."

"I wonder if there's any crumpet around."

We went to bed early and spent the next day doing very little and keeping away from one another between occasional swims in the sea, despite warnings about the current and high tides. We had dinner together, fried fish again, and were on our third bottle of Three Fountains when a man wearing a 1970s suit with a wide lapel and fat tie came loping towards us, tall, handsome with a shy, wry smile on his face. Big hair, forested eyebrows, thin sensual lips and a swollen nose. I should have recognised him from a distance, before he could see my features, from the silhouette. Everything about his slow walk and the nonchalant turn of the head, first to the left, then to the right, said: I am either a moody model or a vampire. But I could see no good, immediate reason why Robert Pattinson, aka Edward Cullen of 'Twilight' fame, would be there, on that beach, in the middle of a war zone.

Pattinson walked straight over to the table and put his hand out to Torment.

"You know who I am," he said. "And I don't know who you are. Please, don't get up."

Torment looked at me for support. "I am Chris Torment," he said boorishly, as if Pattinson were the first person in his life not to recognise him.

"That doesn't help at all, I'm afraid."

I stood up, wondering what Joe had to do with this appearance.

"Chris, it must be the light, or the beer," I said. "This is Robert Pattinson. *The* Robert Pattinson." They shook hands. "And this is Chris Torment, as I'm sure you know really."

Now it was Torment's turn to stand. "Of course, Robin, welcome to..."

"Robert."

"Robert. Excuse me."

"But you can call me RPattz. What's your name?"

We all sat down, Pattinson astride a white plastic chair the wrong way round, like a cop from a TV show.

"Okay," Torment said, ignoring the invitation for a second introduction. "And what on earth are you doing here, Our Pa...?"

"RPattz. It's what millions upon millions of teenage girls around the world call me."

"I see."

"What do they call you, granddad?"

Torment did not register for a while. Then he looked again at me for support. I had a few choice names of what people might call him in my head. *Fop Pants* was the first to spring to mind.

"What do they call me?"

"Yeah, when you're not out mowing your lawn or getting your hearing aid fixed."

"I'm sorry, but..."

"Don't be sorry. You can't help being deaf. I said *when you're not out mowing your lawn or getting you hearing aid fixed.*"

"I heard what you said. Look, who do you think you are?"

"A gigantic movie star half your age. Who do you think *you* are?"

"Who am I? I was making serials for the BBC before you were a glint in your father's eye."

"Oh right."

"Haven't seen any of your films yet myself. Not too big on the whole vampire *genre*, quite honestly. All a bit pale and listless."

"That's okay. I haven't seen any of your films either. In fact, I haven't heard of any of your films. Name one for me please."

"Name one?"

"If you wouldn't mind."

"You mean just off the top of my head?"

"Well, either you name one or we all sit around looking at each other. Or I'll talk to this silent type over here." Pattinson nodded in my direction. "Chris Torment. The name's familiar, but I don't know any of your old stuff."

"Old stuff?"

"Hold on. Weren't you in 'Colditz' back in the eighties?"

"Sorry?"

"Or was that the sixties? Ha ha ha."

"Look, I am currently making 'I Love Hong Kong'. With Panda Koo, if you don't mind."

"I *do* mind, my old China. She's lovely! She's *hot*. And young enough to be your daughter. You should be ashamed of yourself. Weren't you in some Robin Hood bollocks my dad used to watch?"

"I don't know your dad."

"Back in the eighties. Slotted in between 'Kojak' and 'Dad's Army'. Or was that the seventies? I don't know. I wasn't born. Would have had better things to do if I had been."

"Look, you obnoxious little wimp."

"Ooh, that hurts."

"In my day, we would show some respect to our elders."

"So you did have a day, then. That's good. But your elders, that's a tough one. Gene Kelly? Stewart Granger? Sir Ralph Richardson? You reckon there's any totty on this island? Feeling a bit deprived."

"That's what Chris was just asking," I butted in, trying to ease the tension as Torment looked ready to explode.

Pattinson did one of his slow turns of the head to look at me as the waiter arrived with beer.

"So the silent type speaks."

"My name is Hadley. I'm a journalist."

"Well, you don't have to worry," Pattinson said, flicking back a strand of hair from over his left eye. "If there wasn't any totty before I arrived, there will be now. *Hey, hey, hey.* Cheers."

He lifted the bottle to his lips and replaced it slowly on the table, looking at Torment with pouting lips. So this was the diffident superstar who doesn't like fame and likes to keep his private life private? Now he's talking about totty and going *hey, hey, hey*? Something was amiss.

Out of the darkness came three more men. Again there was the big hair, the swagger, the diffidence. All three looked like... Robert Pattinson. I looked at the original, sitting and snarling at Torment.

"You're not Robert Pattinson at all, are you?" Torment said.

"What?" It was an insolent, provocative response with no final consonant. It was a yob's response and it made the three other Robert Pattinsons giggle.

"Who are you, sonny?" This was Torment. An angry Fop Pants sensing it was time to get even, and setting himself up for more of the same.

"I'm going to be the next fucking James Bond, mate," the first Pattinson said. "You ask Joe."

"Joe?"

It came out as easy as anything. Which way was this little show going now? The mention of Joe's name when he wasn't around was becoming more and more menacing.

"Yeah, Joe. The American guy who has been helping to arrange the competition. What do you think we're all doing here?"

"What competition is that, sonny?" Torment asked.

"Pops doesn't know. Along the beach, at the next hotel. They're having a Robert Pattinson look-alike competition."

"What on earth for?" said Torment. "This is a war zone, for heaven's sake."

"Well, it's not much of a crowd, I'll admit. In fact, only a few people in the audience and they were all Chinese."

"Chinese?" He had my attention.

"Except for Joe, of course, who seems very excited about the whole thing."

"Of course I was excited," said the man with a ponytail as he joined our table. "Hi there, Hadley." Joe, looking like an old boxer, stretched out his hand to me and then Torment. "And you are Chris Torment. Boy oh boy, what a strange meeting this is. Forgive me, I saw you both at the junk party."

"I remember," I said. "What are you doing here?" I meant, what in the name of jiggy-jiggy are you doing here.

"What am I doing? A bit of this, a bit of that. Right now I'm putting on the first ever Robert Pattinson look-alike contest to be held in this part of the world."

"Why?" Torment asked again. "I'm surprised anyone has even heard of Robert Pattinson in this part of the world."

"Have they heard of you?" This was Joe.

"Well, of course. But that's not the point. They're not having a Chris Torment look-alike competition. Not that I've heard of anyway."

"We could always try one."

"We could try. But the judges wouldn't know what Chris Torment looks like." This came from one of the new Robert Pattinsons. "Anyone could win."

"It wouldn't matter," another said. "As long as they've all got cardigans and hearing aids."

"Guys, guys," Joe said, a big smile on his face. "Take it easy on the old timer. Tell you what, head back to the hotel and relax. Put the drinks on my tab. I got business to discuss here."

"You thinking of opening an old people's home, Joe?" the first Pattinson said.

"Okay, that's it." Torment jumped up from his chair and made a dash round the table. Joe casually put an arm out and grabbed him around the waist, stopping him in his tracks.

"Beat it," he said to the standing Pattinsons, who turned and trotted away. The original got up slowly and joined them.

"Nice work, Joe," he said. "Try to have a good evening."

"Don't mind them," Joe said after the Pattinsons had gone. "They're young. I like that first one. He's got balls."

"Not if I had anything to do with it," Chris said, sitting back down. "The young... scamp."

"He's just 23 and he's convinced he's going to be the next James Bond. Sooner, rather than later."

"Give me strength," said Torment. "Shouldn't he at least wait until he starts shaving?"

The waiter, wearing a bandana, arrived with drinks. I was interested in how Joe planned to move things along.

"I guess he'll have to wait a while. But Chris, is it true they may have you lined up to be the next James Bond?"

Joe had a big smile on his face. No holds barred. This was

what he called theatrical flourish?

"If I could have a penny for every time someone has asked me that."

Joe was smiling broadly still, his fingers drumming the table.

"A penny for your thoughts then."

"Well, between you and me. My chances aren't looking too shabby at the moment." I noticed that barmy old superiority returning to Torment's voice.

"Not too shabby. How very English. So you've been approached?"

"I wouldn't say that, but..."

"Well, what would you say? Obviously you'd be interested." Joe was still smiling. What had happened to the code of conduct? Joe leant forward and said conspiratorially: "And by the look of the company you were keeping on the junk the other night, you've already got your Bond girl set up." He winked at Torment and slapped his knee.

"Well, I'm not sure I appreciate..."

"What are you talking about? She was all over you." Torment glanced uneasily at me as Joe continued. "But between you and me, I reckon you're a bit too intellectual for the part."

"Well don't count your chickens. I may surprise you yet."

"A bit soft and lily white. And those guys had a point. I mean, you ain't no spring chicken no more. I believe they're looking for someone fresh. Not David Beckham..."

"David Beckham?"

"I said not David Beckham. But someone they could build on, someone like him A bit younger, maybe."

"Look, my friend. I am not sure who you are or how you seem to know so much about the film industry, let alone the James Bond franchise. But there's a lot more to the process of finding the next James Bond than just finding some cute footballer."

"No shit."

"They consider many, many different things. The class of

Englishness, for one."

"Sean Connery is Scottish."

"The class of Britishness then."

"No, I don't think so. Pierce Brosnan is Irish."

"Also the sense of gravitas."

"Gravitas? Pretentious? Moi? You mean superiority, I think."

"Look, who are you? What do you do? How come you think you know so much? You're running some hotel game show, for heaven's sake."

"I do a lot of things." Joe pulled out a cutting from his jacket pocket. "Funnily enough, I happen to know the latest odds on who is going to be the next James Bond. Coming in at ninth at 10/1 is yours truly, Chris Torment. Coming in at 200/1 is David Beckham."

"David Beckham?"

"Two hundred to one. Don't be concerned. My point, Mr Torment, is that there are a few bright sparks above you."

"Read the list," Torment said.

"I can't."

"Oh go on."

"I can't."

"Why can't you? You've got it in your hand, for heaven's sake."

Joe looked at the newspaper cutting. "I could read this out to you if you like..."

"Go on."

"...but it's got nothing to do with what we are talking about."

"I don't understand."

"That was just a coincidence, you see – my pulling this out of my pocket and my saying I knew the odds on who was going to be the next James Bond." Torment was confused and his mouth was open. "Don't let it worry you, please. This article is about the island." Joe put it back in his pocket. "Apparently it's full of snakes. You should watch yourselves."

We heard some splashing from offshore and I got out of my chair and looked out to sea. Not enough light to see, but I could hear the thump of a load of rowlocks.

"Who are you, man?" Torment asked Joe. "What do you do? What are you doing here?"

"I've done a lot of things. Often on the entertainment side. Oh come on, I'm just *teasing* you." Joe leant over and slapped Torment's leg again. "Don't mind me."

Torment flinched. "Often on the entertainment side. What does that mean?"

"I've been instrumental in casting. Hence the Robert Pattinson show. You never know who's going to turn up. I've also been involved in entrepreneurial projects and I do a whole bunch of other bits and pieces. Imports and exports. And I can do occasionally dynamic things. Pyrotechnics, for instance. I can do some now, if you like."

"What are you talking about, man?"

"Raise your left arm. And put your heart into it. Punch your left fist into the air. Go on. I will show you some of my powers."

Torment put on a schoolboy pout but did as he was told. Nothing happened.

"That didn't work," Joe said. "I want you to try again."

"Oh please."

"Punch your left fist into the air, followed immediately by your right."

"I don't want…"

"Just do it."

Chris sighed, stood up and did an athletic punch in the air with his left fist, John Travolta style, and then, head down, threw another with the right.

The Disco Groove Nite Hut exploded into fragments of bamboo which showered the entire hotel. The sound system shattered and a white plastic chair whipped dangerously past the waiter with the bandana. We found ourselves without a table.

Monkeys and parrots were screaming all along the coast.

"What the fuck was that?" said Torment, now spread-eagled on the red pavestones, looking out to sea.

"Whatever you do, don't mention Shirley Bassey," Joe warned. He had a mischievous smile on his face.

"What?"

"The singer. Shirley Bassey. I'm being serious. Don't do it."

"Who in their right mind, do you think, here and now, would feel the urge to mention Shirley Bassey?"

"Too loud, you complete fucker. I said don't…"

There was heavy gunfire, aimed at the Jungle Wing of the Lagoon Beach Hotel. Windows were shattering, chips of wood were flying, television sets were exploding. Whoever was doing the shooting now started aiming closer to us. At least seven Robert Pattinson types were running in all directions with their heads down.

"Head for the trees!"

Four shots rang out quickly from behind me. Torment and I crawled over to the cover of the palm trees. I remembered being taught on a hostile environment course that any tree you could put your arms around probably wasn't going to be enough to stop a bullet. I saw Joe sitting in the same seat, grinning and unmoved.

"Who is this guy?" I muttered to myself.

Then there was silence. Or rather just the sound of the sea, as though the shooting had whipped up the waves, along with the screaming monkeys. I edged my face around the tree, too high up on the beach to see any boats against the skyline. I looked towards the hotel. Joe was not visible but then, like a cockroach, he re-appeared at the edge of the light. He looked about him and sat down again. He raised his glass in a salute. No, it was another signal. At once, gunfire started from inside the hotel. Joe stood up and ran up the beach towards us, sticking his tongue out like a naughty boy.

"What's going on?" I shouted. "What are you doing?"

"We're leaving now. Some guys are ransacking the front office as we speak."

"Where are we going?" Torment asked.

"To another island."

Joe ran at a crouch, Torment and I following close behind, down to the sea where a long boat with an outboard motor was waiting. Joe looked pleased with himself as we climbed unsteadily aboard. Joe pushed the boat out over the lapping waves and hopped in. Inside were a fishing rod and a hurricane lamp. The sudden burst of activity made me want to throw up.

"Where are we going?" Torment asked again. "Joe, who *are* you?"

The engine was noisy and smoky, but no one started shooting. Joe was standing in the stern with his hand on a long tiller. We were heading round to the far side of the island.

"Can someone please explain what is going on?" Torment said. "Who are we running from and where are we going? How do you know we aren't running straight into them?"

Joe looked in complete control. "Hush now," was all he said.

HALF AN HOUR later, Joe turned off the outboard and let the waves take the boat into a small bay. We climbed out and he pulled the boat on to the sand, covering it with camouflage netting, and led the way up a sandy path. We were circling a smooth, symmetrical hill like a burial mound. I could smell dry grass. It smelt more like Cornwall than the tropics. Up ahead was a long bungalow surrounded by hydrangeas. Through a gap in some fir trees to the left, I saw a helicopter. Joe knocked on the front door, which was opened immediately by a man in a Hawaiian shirt. Joe went inside and disappeared through a side door, while Torment and I were led into a big, comfortable room with rattan furniture, cushions on the floor and a skylight. I could smell cigar smoke. The man in the Hawaiian shirt sat at the far end of the room and said nothing, but he kept catching my eye. I sat on a sofa and picked up a magazine from the glass-topped coffee table. On closer inspection, I realised it wasn't a magazine, but an index of the DVDs that lined the wall.

Joe returned and sat at the head of the table. He had changed into a t-shirt with 'Ben Hur' written on the front.

"Okay, sorry about that. Hadley, this is our temporary new home." Joe gestured proudly at the DVDs. "I told you I did a lot of filming. What do you think of the place?"

"It looks very nice."

"Very nice. Okay, someone's bringing whisky. Look, Chris, I have to level with you. I haven't been completely honest about why you are here. Or why any of us are here."

Where was he going with this?

"What on earth is going on?" Chris asked, looking from Joe to me. "Who were those people shooting at us? I demand to know. Why have you brought us here?"

"Of course. I'll tell you everything. Chris, as a professional actor, I hope you won't be offended by this..."

"What are you talking about, man?"

"But it's because you are such a professional that I can tell you what's really going on."

"For heaven's sake, get on with it!"

Joe took a deep breath. "To use English terminology, you are a complete berk."

"I beg your pardon?"

"You can beg what you like. I am not going to apologise. You are a berk of the highest order, but you are a berk I can work with."

"You can't say..."

"Yes I can. Please let me explain. You mustn't take this personally. All actors are berks. I want you to sit back, enjoy your drink and let me explain. Will you let me do that?"

"But you can't go around..."

"Will you let me do that?"

Fop Pants sat back with a sulk, folding his arms across his chest.

"That's good. Now let me explain a little of what I do. I film everyone and everything. I film people even when they don't know they are being filmed." I looked around the walls and sure enough, there in the far corner, was the camera. "Some of the stuff I have done is being used in your new movie."

" 'I Love Hong Kong'?"

"Exactly. Adolf Lee is a big fan of my work, and I'm a big fan of his. I film people all over the place. It's a bit of an obsession of mine. Then, when it comes to making a movie, I can choose scenes out of a box. I mix and match it, with new software I have developed myself. It's like an artist choosing his paints. You can have the same actor in a movie as a child *and* as an old man or woman. Think about that. No special effects, no makeup. The same person. I can *create* an entire person."

"But I don't understand," said Torment. "How would you know what to film? How would you know what film was going to be made twenty, thirty years later? The idea is preposterous. How would you know the child would even grow up to be an actor?"

"Chris..."

"I mean," Torment went on, encouraged. He stood up and started pacing the floor. "Take a movie like 'Giant'. Rock Hudson and James Dean are young and then they get old. As does Elizabeth Taylor. Are you saying you could do that?"

"Well of course not, but..."

"Well, there you go. Who's the berk now?"

"I am talking about a completely new concept of making films. You will see some of it in your movie. You wait."

"But the whole idea's just silly. Hadley, help me out here."

"Let me put it this way, Chris," said Joe. "I was in a supermarket in LA a few weeks ago and I had a shopping cart. Embedded in the handle bar was a calculator, so you could add prices up as you went around the shop, seeing how much you were spending. Are you following me so far?"

"Yes, but..."

"What do you think about that?"

"Useful, I suppose."

"Useful. Exactly. Now, suppose I said to you – no, suppose I *gave* you a present. A shiny, pocket-sized calculator. But this calculator was special, because it came with a fucking great supermarket trolley stuck next to the percentage key. In between the percentage key and the square root. What would you say to that?"

"A bit unwieldy, I suppose."

"Not just unwieldy. Complete fucking waste of space. Am I right?"

"Can't disagree." Fop Pants looked at me for support. The look in his eyes said: Joe is completely off his supermarket trolley and if we run for it now, we might just make it.

"I think what Joe is trying to say," I ventured, struggling with the image of Joe in a supermarket, looking for the bargain of the day in the cold meats section, "is that there are different ways of looking at things."

"*Totally* different. You will both see what I'm talking about, right here on this very island. Totally unusual ways. Who ever heard of a calculator with a trolley attached?"

Torment was not convinced. "So you're filming us. What does that have to do with our being here?"

"The second purpose is of more immediate importance. I am working to ensure that the next series of Bond films is a rip-roaring success. That's my job."

Torment and I stared at Joe, who pulled out a cigar which in turn prompted an image from my childhood, a James Bond annual my dad had given me for Christmas when I was about ten. It had full-page pictures of Sean Connery, including one from

'Goldfinger' of him leaning against his Aston Martin wearing a grey trilby and smoking a cigar, and one from 'Thunderball' wearing a very un-macho one-piece towel suit. Between the pictures there were short Bond stories, most dating back to the years after the war in an unexotic England. But what I remembered most was the front cover – round the edges were little silhouette motifs of Bond fighting someone off with flailing arms which, if viewed at arm's length and through squinted eyes, looked like complicated Chinese characters.

"I'm sorry to tell you Chris," Joe said, "but there is no way we can let you be the next James Bond – this is not me speaking. I am just the messenger."

Joe spent a long time lighting the cigar, puffing noisily. I was drumming my fingers against my thigh and feeling, for the first time, a little sorry for Torment, a lamb being led to the slaughter. So he was ambitious. So he was a bit of a prima donna and a prick. And a bully. And an arrogant waste of space. And he may or may not have bonked Maria. And my sister. Well, there were pricks all over the world – surgeons, teachers, wire journalists even. They would all get their come-uppance, one way or another. It didn't mean they should be subjected to a sadistic game of cat and mouse. I opened my mouth to say something, but Joe put a hand up to silence me.

"Like I said, Chris, there is no way we can let you be the next James Bond… without toughening you up a bit."

"Yet again, I fail to understand."

"Just look at me as a freelance casting agent."

Torment took a while to register this information. He got up and started to walk around the room again. His shirt was untucked at the back and his casual blue trousers were caked in dust.

"Let me get this straight," he said. "Are you one of those people…?"

Joe put his cigar in his mouth and grinned. "I have no idea

what you're talking about." His voice was muffled by the huge sizzling wad of tobacco.

Torment sat down and promptly stood up again. He was pointing at Joe and mouthing words. But they weren't coming out. Then he pointed at me and mouthed some more words. "Oh my god. Hadley, you know what this means?"

"It's unbelievable," I said. "Completely unbelievable. I can't believe my ears."

"Thanks, man. You're right, Joe. I must get in shape. I'll start with a gentle jog along the beach in the morning. But when do I start? Which movie?"

"Hold your horses," Joe said. "I haven't finished my story."

"You want to toughen me up a bit. I understand. I'm no spring chicken. It's my abs, I know."

"It's got nothing to do with your *abs*. In fact, I don't like that word. It's lazy American English and I don't want you using it again."

"Well, excuse..."

"Do you understand?"

"Well..."

"Do you understand?"

"Yes," Torment said after a pause.

"I want to toughen *you* up and I want to do it right here on this island. The visit to the monsoon damage can wait. I want you to leave this island looking and feeling a new man. Lean, mean and hard."

"That's my abs."

"If you use that word again, I will take you down."

"But you said before I was too soft and lily white!"

"And I was right. But I was talking about you as a person. I was talking metaphorically. Do you know what that means?"

"I think so."

"I am talking about the whole damn package."

"Well, if you're talking about the 'whole package', why didn't you say so?" Torment hazarded a laugh.

Joe turned towards me and the look in his eye said it all: *this man is hopeless, my mission to fuck him over is virtuous and the chances of a violent ending are high and rising.*

"Chris," Joe said, putting an arm around his shoulders. "Chris, Chris, Chris."

"Joe, Joe, Joe."

"Try to get it into your head that we need to get the whole world on your side as the next 007."

"You don't think the whole world is on my side?"

"Not yet. Not the *whole* world. But I have, how can I put it, great expectations."

"Well, bring it on. Let's do it. Actually, what do I have to do?"

"Firstly, I want you to try to think before you speak."

"Think?"

"Yes, if you could. I want you to become a person who doesn't say things like 'ooh, where's the crumpet' and 'look at my package' and 'bring it on'. Do you think you could try that?"

"You mean now?"

"If you could start now, that would be terrific."

"Then what?"

"Well, we have done some pre-planning here, my colleagues and I. And the plan, now that your Hong Kong movie is almost in post-production, is to lock you up and keep you out of sight for a while."

"Here?"

"We were thinking an outhouse, if that's okay."

"An outhouse?"

"Yes. It'll be like a dark cell. Don't forget I will be filming everything."

"Wow. You must think me awfully ungrateful."

"Not at all. Think about what I said and come back with any questions any time. Or ideas. I like ideas."

"Okay. I'm an ideas man myself."

"Ah."

"Let's do it. Bring it on."

"Yes. Let's do it."

Joe pressed a buzzer and two men wearing khaki uniforms appeared. They led Chris out, followed by the man in the Hawaiian shirt who closed the door quietly behind him, but not before winking at me.

"I am going to see you soon, right?" Torment said to us both.

"Of course. Don't worry."

CHAPTER TWELVE

THE DOOR CLOSED and Joe sighed loudly through pursed lips. He walked across the room, sat down on the sofa and put his head in his hands.

" 'Bring it on'," he said. "Why can't this guy get it? I hope you are starting to realise how important my job is, Hadley."

"So now you want me to write stories about him being toughened up?"

"Just write what you see. Look at it this way, at least he won't be screwing around with your girlfriend any more."

"What's that supposed to mean?"

Joe turned to the man in the Hawaiian shirt who had resumed his position at the end of the room. "Reggie, have we got the latest?"

Reggie nodded, looking sadly at me. What was it with this guy?

"Good," Joe said. "Put it on."

"Right you are."

"We're going to see a movie?" I asked.

"Yeah, right," said Joe. "'Great Expectations'. First off, do you know Reggie? Introduce yourself, Reggie."

Reggie stood up, wiping his palms down the back of his trousers.

"It is me, I am afraid, Mr Arnold. Reggie, your stringer. Reggie Waverly. I am afraid I lost my faith. I am sorry."

"Your faith in what?"

"Let's all sit down and talk about that some other time," Joe said. "Reggie, put it on."

Waverly looked along a line of DVDs, pulled one down and put it in the machine. I just had time to make out some hand-written title on the cover. Two words. Arnold, Hadley? I couldn't see clearly.

"One more thing, Hadley," Joe said. "Forget about Chen and his Chinese group."

"You mean they aren't involved?"

"Not any more. I don't need them. Watch the movie."

Joe turned to the screen which flickered for a few seconds through a home video of countryside and hills in the distance. It wasn't until I saw a minibus pass that I realised it was Hong Kong. It was Kam Tin. The cameraman was outside the Honest Bar, in the car park, in daylight. He was doing a crude 360-degree sweep of the hills at the beginning of the Lam Tsuen valley, then the road leading away to my village, a string of duck farms and one or two Nepalese restaurants. There was the car-wrecking yard filled with Japanese taxis. Not just Japanese-made taxis, but bodyworks of taxis with Japanese inscriptions saying taxi and giving details of fares. I had never figured out what they were doing there but imagined there was a story in it (American cars in the Fens, Japanese taxis in the New Territories). A double-decker bus had broken down just in front. Its engine was open to the elements and the driver was standing with his hands on his hips looking pissed off.

Now the cameraman was walking up to the bar. The door was opened for him by a grinning ah-Fei looking proud and ridiculous. The bar was empty. The cameraman sat down in the corner and surveyed the scene. There were no customers. Not even the bloke at the bar with the long hair who looked like a famous cricketer. The focus and exposure were screwed up each time the cameraman panned past the door and the sunlight outside. Then someone was wiping down his table and a huge face came out of focus into the picture.

"What would you like to drink, sir?"

Suddenly in focus, it was Maria. Staring into the camera. She stepped back. She was wearing a tee-shirt and no bra and the shortest, lowest skirt I had never seen. She was trying not to giggle.

"Maria," I said under my breath. Joe turned to look at me and nodded and half pointed at the screen.

The cameraman didn't say anything and Maria turned and walked back to the bar. She was being deliberately provocative. The skirt barely covered her bum. She was being jaunty. The man put the camera, still running, down on the table. It was pointed, at an angle, at the seat next to him. All I could see of the cameraman was a dark sleeve, which flitted in and out of picture. Then there was a bit of commotion, the table moved, and someone sat down. It was Maria. The camera was looking directly at her skirt.

"There's a game I like to play," she said. Her hand was moving up and down her thigh. "I like to play it with married men only."

The camera didn't move, the cameraman didn't say anything.

"I say to them: 'What's the quickest way you can think of to find out if I'm wearing panties.' Then I wait. Not very long usually. The most loyal husband maybe fifteen seconds..."

The table shook and a big hand grabbed Maria's leg. The camera went clank and there was Torment's grinning face.

The film stopped. Neither Joe nor Reggie said a word.

"They make a nice couple," I said after a while.

"Don't blame her," said Joe. "He's a handsome movie star and she's a..."

"She's a what?"

"I'm sorry, Hadley. Seems to me they were made for each other. You know what this handsome movie star does back in your country? He calls the picture editor of the Sun each time he sees a page three girl he likes. He gets the agent's number and wham bam, she's in his bed within two hours. That's the kind of life he leads, and he's not the only one. That's the kind of power famous people have. This should help to set the mood for your colour pieces about our mutual friend."

"How am I going to file my stories?"

"There's a satellite phone in your room. The internet is still down and we don't have any cell phones, but we're working on it."

"I'm going to make some calls."

I went to my room and shut the door. I stared out the window and thought about Torment in a dank cell thinking his career was on the up and up. I thought about Torment making love to Maria. Maybe in Joe's apartment. "I'm not in love," I said aloud, imagining a life composed entirely of song titles and lines from movies. Joe could engineer it somehow.

I took the satellite phone outside and waited for it to lock on to a signal. I called my parents' home in Sotobech where it was about seven in the evening and got my sister's Edinburgh number, fending off questions from my mother about my new-found fame.

"Pamela?"

"Yes?"

"Pamela, this is Hadley. I'm calling from Macho."

"Hadley! Where are you?"

"Macho."

"How exciting! We've been reading about you."

"Really? What have you been reading? Who's we?"

"About you at that party in Hong Kong where you saved Chris's life. You're famous over here. What are you doing in Bermuda?"

"I'm not in Bermuda." Why was she calling him Chris? Torment was the name even my mother used when she referred to the only boy from Halfords to "make good" in the world. "I'm on business. Covering the war in Macho. Pamela, I'm using a very expensive satellite phone link and I can't stay on. But there is something important I have to ask."

"Is it about the beet farm?"

"The beet farm? No, not the beet farm. It's about Torment."

There was a significant pause, the sound of the receiver changing hands. My heart was beating fast. "Pamela, did you hear me?"

"Yes. What about him?"

"Well he's been saying some pretty crazy things recently, some of them involving you."

"Go on."

I cleared my throat. "He said you and he had a thing together, years ago. When you were about seventeen. He said he came to Sotobech, and you were there alone, and, basically, one thing led to another..."

"Why did he tell you that?"

"Because he's a malevolent arsehole, that's why. He's a vicious, self-important..."

"He said he would never tell anyone."

"What? Are you saying he wasn't lying?"

"Well he lied to me, obviously, the shit."

"So it happened?"

"Yes, Hadley, it happened. Really, you can be so precious. I don't want to know what he said, but it happened. It was a magic moment."

"You bonked Torment? After all he did to me? And you call it a magic moment? This is what mum means by 'making good' in the world?"

I was suddenly aware of the distance these words were travelling, bouncing off some orbiting space station and being picked up on Mars where everyone was having a really good laugh out of their bottoms. The line went fuzzy and then I was only picking up odd words. "Torment... Halfords... really enormous."

"Pamela, you're breaking up. I don't know if you can hear me but I'm hanging up. Thanks for nothing."

I hung up and the phone rang. A distant constellation asking for more.

"Hello, is that Arnold Harley?"

"Power to bonk. No it's not."

There was a pause. "I'm sorry, this is Eric from Camden Radio in London. We are trying to trace Arnold Harley."

"He's not here."

"Oh."

"I am Hadley Arnold. Can I help?"

"I do apologise. They told us you were still up."

"I'm still up, yes. Who told you? How did you get this number?"

"I'm not quite sure actually."

"Well, what do you want?"

"We were wondering if you could spare us a couple of minutes on our Asia Focus programme. We could take you there live in a few minutes. Sorry for such short notice, but you know how it is."

"How is it?"

"We heard about some trouble near where you are."

"Nearby. But I haven't heard any news for hours. You'll have to make the questions general."

"Okay. No problem. Thanks for helping us out. Let me get the pronunciation right. Hadley Arnold."

"That's right."

"And you're in the middle of the war zone, near Tarragona."

"Tarragona?"

"Please hold on."

I heard a scuffle of voices and a hand put across the phone and then Eric was back on the line.

"Sorry, you're not *the* Hadley Arnold?"

"I am Hadley Arnold. I'm not sure what you mean. I'm not in Spain."

"You're the guy that saved Chris Torment's life, right?"

"Not exactly."

I heard Eric put his hand over the phone again and say: "What a shit." He came back on the line but was not as friendly as before.

"Okay, tell me if you can hear me clearly," he said.

"I can hear you. I'm not in Tarragona."

"I don't care where you are. Don't mess around, okay? I'm going to leave you with the show. You will hear Susan sign off a guest, there will be a time check and a bit of the jingle. He'll introduce you, and then you'll be on live. Is that clear?"

"Susan's a he? I'm not in Spain."

"I'm leaving you with the show."

I listened and waited. Familiar night-time British commercial radio sounds. I imagined deserted motorways and people smoking cigarettes and stamping their feet in the cold outside service stations. I saw the West End streets after all the bars had closed and dodgy people standing in shop doorways, near casinos, waiting for fun. When fun didn't arrive, they stood in shop doorways waiting for mini-cabs. They didn't arrive either. I thought about Torment's power to bonk and wondered what line the bastard had used on my sister. My sister! And he wasn't even famous then. I wanted a gin and tonic. I heard Susan.

"And now we are going over live to the South Pacific Macho Island where the ethnic war has been raging for donkeys with all sorts of mayhem. On the line from the frontline in Tamaranda is Shrubs's man in deep doo-doo, Harley Armwood. Harley, are you there?"

I allowed a long pause. "Hello, mum?"

"Hello, is that Harley Armwood?"

"Hello, mum?"

"Hello Harley. Good to have you Cool on Camden. Harley, tell us, we've been hearing dreadful stories about bombs in Colombia, tourists pulling out in droves, the economy in tatters. But

I hear there's a lighter side to all this. What's it all about?"

I thought a while. A lighter side to all this? In Colombia? I took a deep breath.

"Hello, mum?"

"Oh dear, we seem to have a crossed line..."

"Hello. This is Hadley Arnold."

"Hadley. Welcome. We have you Cool on Camden. I don't know whether you caught the question."

"Not a word."

"It's just that we here in London have been hearing awful things about the fighting in Sri Lanka in recent years, but thankfully we hear there is a lighter side."

"I'm sorry, Susan, but can't think of one actually. There has been some sporadic violence here in Macho, but that is nothing out of the ordinary for this sun-baked archipelago where violence is pretty much, though not so much, endemic and entrenched after years of ethnic and civil unrest. As it is on the mainland."

"Wow. Well, we hear that while some people may have been having a tough time of it, it's onion soup on the house in all the top hotels."

I frowned and looked into the receiver. I banged it against a palm tree.

"Hello, Hadley. Are you there?"

"Yes, I'm sorry. Could you repeat the question?"

"Yes. The papers here have picked up on the story that while some people may have been having a tough time of it in, um, near you, it's onion soup on the house in all the top hotels."

The penny dropped. The onion story. I tried to remember my intro.

"Well, you're not far wrong there, Susan. It appears a ship carrying a load of red onions was barred entry from one of the islands and the skipper decided to dump his load overboard and look for trade elsewhere."

"Oh no. What happened?"

"Oh yes. Well, put it this way, Susan, the British tourists are not the only things lying on the beaches turning red and peeling."

"Ha, ha, ha. Wow, what a story. You mean the onions are being washed up on the beaches?"

"That's right, Susan. In their hundreds. What a load of... onions. All along the golden beaches of this tropical paradise."

"And they're peeling?"

"Well, I expect so."

"You said they were."

"They are."

"So you saw them. And I hear that the locals are showing some pretty amazing entrepreneurial spirit?"

"That's right, Susan. They've been gathering up the onions and selling them at roadside stores, and making a hefty profit into the bargain."

"And it's onion soup on all the hotel menus tonight, right?"

"I expect so, but I'd plump for the melon for starters. The soup could be a tad salty."

"Ha ha ha. Okay, that sounds like good advice from the tropics. But swap me some of that equatorial sunshine for some salty soup any time."

"Yes." I didn't know what he was talking about. "But the onions are really 'Macho ado about nothing' as there has been a war raging on the mainland and only last night..."

"I also see, Hadley, from a piece of paper just handed to me, that you're the Hadley Arnold who saved Chris Torment's life in Hong Kong a few weeks back."

"Well, that's not strictly..."

"And now we are hearing rumours he's been kidnapped near you?"

Where did they get that from? "Kidnapped? I haven't heard that. But I am here. I mean, I will find out what's going on."

"Our man in deep doo-doo and he hasn't got a clue. Extraordinary. But there we have to leave the tropics and return to grimy old London where we hear a coal truck has shed its load at the north end of Tottenham Court Road..."

"Hadley?"

"Yes?"

"It's all over. You're back with Eric. Thanks for that onion bollocks."

"Thanks for what?"

"For that bollocks about the onions."

"You mean that's it?"

"Bugger off."

The line went dead. Confused and angry, I hung up and dialled my office.

"Rodney?"

"Hadley? What the hell are you doing and how come we haven't had a word on Torment? It's all over the internet."

"Yes, thank you, I'm fine."

"What?"

"What's all over the internet?"

"That Torment has been kidnapped. He is being held in a cell by the same people who tried to kill him."

"Who's saying it? What's the source?"

"A rebel source who didn't want to be identified."

"I bet he didn't."

"What? Hadley, can you match this?" To match a story in agency journalese is to get your own version and draw a veil over the fact that the opposition got there before you. "Hadley, are you there?"

"I'm here."

"Can you get a matcher?" Silly agency journalese again. Like a phoner, which was similar to what my boss and I were having right now. The habit dated back to the days of telegrams which were paid for by the word and the idea was to save money. "*I have finished my story and am off to the pub*" would become "*bar-*

wards".

"I can do better. I can knock it down."

"Seriously?"

"Seriously."

"Well, what have you got?"

"What do you mean, what have I got? In terms of hard currency? Tropical diseases?"

"Don't be a prat. What have you got to give us?"

"I've just been talking to the bastard. He's here with me. Can Fagin take copy?"

"I'll put him on."

The adrenalin was running now. Fuck Baxter. And Joe. Just watch your foreign correspondent in full flight. Bollocks to all of you.

"Hadley, it's Fagin."

"Bollocks."

"What?"

"Fagin, I'm sorry. I was thinking aloud. Baxter questioning whether or not I am serious. Fuck him."

"Are you okay out there?"

"Yes, thanks."

"So what have you got?"

"Okay. First tell me what the word is about what happened to Torment."

"I can read it to you. This is from the Hong Kong Express website. Their own story. I haven't seen the agencies or anyone else with it yet."

"Baxter said it was all over the internet!"

"Well he's exaggerating. But London are calling for a matcher. *A Sri Lankan rebel group holding British movie actor Chris Torment hostage said on Tuesday it would kill him unless he renounces all ambition to play James Bond.*"

"Oh boy. Go on."

"Second paragraph. *The Democratic Association for the Libera-*

tion of Jaffna Chinese, a left-wing youth group based on the war-torn island of Macho, took Torment hostage on Friday, just days after the same group tried to kill the actor in Hong Kong."

"It's all lies. Any more?"

"Open quotes. *Torment is well and will not be harmed on the con-dition that he gives up his 007 aspirations,* comma close quotes, *the rebels said in the statement released at their jungle hideout off the main island of Macho.*

"New paragraph, open quotes. *Without the assurance, most spe-cifically that he never plays the part of James Bond in any movies, the actor will die at the end of seven days,* point, close quotes.

"*The DALJC is one of two groups seeking either autonomy or inde-pendence from Sri Lanka. It said Torment's movies promoted western imperialism, defamed minorities and his international exposure had to be,* open quotes, *terminated,* close quotes."

"That's it?"

"That's it."

"Okay, I'll give you a story. He's here with me. He hasn't been kidnapped. Suggest we play it straight, no urgents or bulletins. A simple, non-shouting story which knocks down that report and says he is on an island preparing..." I paused.

"Preparing what?"

Bloody good question. I only had Joe's word on any of this and Joe was from Planet Hula-hoop.

"...preparing for his next movie before visiting the monsoon beaches."

"Okay. Let's have it."

"Fagin. I'll call you back. I have to check a few things first."

I found Joe walking down to the beach with a bag of golf clubs over his shoulder. I explained my call to the office and the newspaper report that Torment had been kidnapped.

"They said the Chinese group had taken him."

Joe poured a dozen balls on to a grassy area under a palm tree and looked out to sea, deciding which club to use. He chose an iron.

"Joe? Did you hear what I said?"

Joe mistimed his shot and sliced the ball thirty yards along the sand.

"My bad," he said.

It was an Americanism I found hugely annoying. "Bad my" would be no less ungrammatical. What was wrong with "whoops"? Joe teed up another ball and hit it gracefully a hundred yards into the waves.

"It would seem that we have a bit of a contradiction on our hands."

"Did you tell the Express he had been taken hostage?"

"That was the original plan. I was going to capture him and knock some sense into him. Maybe subject him to practices of testicular torture that have been neglected since the Middle Ages." He teed up another ball. "But now we are embarking on a more touchy-feely enterprise which may take more time."

Four speed boats spewing out black smoke appeared from the rocky south end of the bay, heading north. I could make out the crew in striped uniforms, about four in each boat, and could hear helicopters.

"Sea Tigers," I said. They were the naval wing of the main rebel group which, unlike the DALJC, some people had actually heard of. The boats had crossed half the bay when two Sri Lankan army helicopters appeared from behind the main house a hundred yards inland, flying low over the beach. No shots were fired. The boats slapped across the waves and out of sight around the peninsula, the helicopters in pursuit.

"Sometimes it's easy to forget we are in a war zone," Joe said, manoeuvring another ball into place with the end of his club. "These parts have known nothing but violence for decades."

"I am going to write a story now. I am going to say that Chris is taking some R&R after his work in Hong Kong and preparing for his next movie."

"What movie might that be?"

"I'll talk to him. See what he wants to say."

"See what he says and then write your story?"

"Yes."

"But you don't want to see what I'm saying?"

"No."

"Because you don't really know who I am or what powers I bring to bear." Joe hit another ball out to sea. "Is that it?"

"I know you work for a company that no one knows about and that you are rich and powerful. That's not really enough. I can't really quote you, can I, Joe? I have no way of describing you."

"So write what you see, except pretend you don't see me."

"Until you do something newsworthy. At the moment you have just made a lot of accusations and threats with nothing to back you up. I could write 'a man with a ponytail who doesn't want Chris Torment to become the next James Bond is toughening up Chris Torment on a beach in the middle of nowhere for his next role as James Bond', but I don't think it would make it through the subs. They would excise the line. They would probably excise me. But before they did that, they would question me and I would have to say 'that's what the man said'. And they would say..."

"What would they say?"

"They would ask me who you were. Except in much more colourful language. And I would say that you know Panda really well and that you live in a nice house on the Peak and that you're involved in the movie business and have lots of money and can make explosions at will. But..."

"But?"

"I wouldn't really be able to answer them."

There were two quick explosions from beyond the peninsula and two air force jets screamed overhead from nowhere. Joe lined up another ball.

"You do what you have to do, Hadley," he said. "It'll all work out in the end."

"Can I speak to Torment?"

Joe shrugged his shoulders. I found Torment sitting on his bed chatting up one of the house staff who was about thirty and had swinging hips. She had brought him a gin and tonic.

"Hadley, this is lovely Linda."

The room was big and short on furniture with a wooden beam across the ceiling. A gecko ran up the wall behind the bed. I said hello to Linda, who was lovely and probably had about ten minutes of her lovely life left before being assailed by a flailing white actor with nothing but visions of totty in the grey matter between his ears.

"Chris, I am going to write a story."

"Good stuff. See you later then."

"Hold on, I don't mean to disturb you, but there is a story out there that you have been taken hostage."

"Hostage?"

"I have no idea who came up with it, but yes. Hostage. Kidnapped by the Chinese rebel group."

Torment turned back to Linda. "Not that I would mind being taken hostage right now and tied up and..."

"Please try to pay attention. Just for a minute. I will write a story saying you *haven't* been taken hostage. Are you with me so far?"

"Okay."

"Well can you give me a quote?"

"Hadley, this really isn't a good time. Can't you make one up?"

"I'd rather not. Tell me that you're happy, relaxed, enjoying quality time after the hardships of the movie with Adolf Lee and the assassination attempt. And that you plan to meet the Chinese rebel group. If it exists."

"Tell them about what Joe is doing. Tell them I'm going to be the next James Bond! Man, you have a scoop on your hands."

"Well, I would rather firm that up with the film people first. Chris? Chris?"

Torment had buried his face in Linda's sarong just below her breasts. I didn't want to see any more. Linda was looking at me with a knowing smile.

"Please give me a quote, Chris, and I'll leave you alone."

There came an unintelligible, muffled noise from Linda's sarong. Nothing usable. Chris lifted his head back for air.

"Say this: I am very happy."

"That's it?"

"Hadley, not now."

"You have to say something about the attempted shooting."

"Do I?"

"*The idea I've been taken hostage is preposterous. I am very happy to be taking time off after the rigours of Hong Kong and the attempt on my life. I want to meet the group that is suspected of wanting to kill me. This island is beautiful, though the explosions are really scary.* How about that?"

"All fine except the last part. You don't want to make me out to be a coward. Not the next James Bond. I am very happy etc etc... and at last I've found some crumpet!"

"Oh lord."

"No, don't say that. How about... and at last some crumpet's found me!"

Back in my room, with little appetite right then for bright, colourful prose, I called up Fagin and gave him my story.

British actor Chris Torment denied a report he had been kidnapped in war-torn north Sri Lanka on Wednesday, saying he was at last enjoying some time off after the attempt on his life in Hong Kong.

A Hong Kong newspaper, quoting an unidentified rebel source, said Torment had been taken hostage by the same group that had tried to kill him and that he had been given just a week to live unless he gave up any ambition to play James Bond.

"The idea I've been taken hostage is preposterous," Torment, always an outside dark horse in the race to become the next James Bond, told Shrubs on Macho Island where he is relaxing before a scheduled visit to communities damaged by disastrous monsoon rains.

Torment was speaking as Sri Lanka Air Force jets battled rebel boats offshore in a war that has lasted two decades.

There was no immediate sign of the Democratic Association for the Liberation of Jaffna Chinese which some say may be a fictitious group, raising questions about the "attempt" on Torment's life.

Torment stars in Adolf Lee's new movie, 'I Love Hong Kong', which has been filming on location in the former British colony in recent weeks. The release date has yet to be released.

"The release date has yet to be released?" said Fagin.

"Can you fix it up? Date of release is unknown. Something like that."

"Okay. Baxter wants a word. Hold on."

"Hadley?"

"Yes, Rodney."

"Look, this is terrific stuff."

"Thank you."

"But you're calling him an outside dark horse. I'm not sure what that is?"

"Say he has an outside chance, then."

"But isn't he a dark horse? Meaning he has a good chance?"

I considered this. "I hope not."

"What?"

"I honestly don't know, Rodney."

"Well, it's good stuff and we look forward to more of the same. Are you safe?"

"I'm fine."

"It sounds like this Chinese group is a put-up job."

"It does."

"We have people on it. Nothing so far. Mentions on the internet are just dodgy blogs. I don't want to touch dodgy blogs."

CHAPTER THIRTEEN

CHRIS TORMENT WAS subjected to a rigorous exercise regime while I wrote stories about the island, about the Sea Tigers, about the local mining industry, the war damage, about Torment's passion for bird watching.

"What's this about birds?" Joe said on the third day on the island.

"Took me by surprise too. He knows everything there is to know about tropical flora and fauna."

"You think that's going to help us achieve our purpose? The fact that he knows a lesser-spotted tree warbler from a tit is going to make one goddam bit of difference? Your stories are not hitting the mark. I want to move more quickly."

The next day at breakfast, while Torment was being marched along the beach to a cross-island assault course which meandered through caves at the next bay, Joe threw down some pictures on the table.

"Your friend has some pretty strange habits," Joe said.

The eight-by-ten black-and-white prints showed Chris hanging upside down by his ankles from the beam above his bed wearing nothing but a loin cloth, sunglasses and a leather belt around his neck. His body was covered in oil.

"My god."

"Pretty damning, right?"

"What is he *doing*?"

"Some depraved asphyxiation sex thing. The man disgusts

me."

"But those dark glasses hide his face a bit. Maybe it's not him."

"Hey, I've got a camera in that cell, all right? Who do you think it is? Errol Flynn?"

I flicked through the prints. In one he was holding the belt tight at a right-angle to his torso, in another he had his hand on his crotch and a big smile on his face.

"Wow."

"Anyway, Shrubs have them."

"How?"

"We're back online. There's a laptop in your room, by the way."

It was all too convenient. I called Baxter.

"Rodney, I hope we haven't used these pictures."

"Not yet. We were waiting for you."

"I don't think they are real. Torment is still here with me. But I am now worried about his safety. For the first time."

"You're worried about the rebels?"

"No. About a strange man involved in the movie business. Nothing I can write."

Chris Torment, on an island no one had ever heard of in the middle of a war no one cared about involving one combatant group which didn't exist, was at risk. Then an attempt was made on Torment's life. I knew it hadn't been successful, because it was Torment who told us the next day. Joe was now driving golf balls from a machine which teed up every shot for him. The cameras were rolling everywhere.

"Some bastard really is trying to kill me," Torment, dressed in an orange sarong, said. "You won't *believe* what I've been through in the last twelve hours. Never mind our fun and games. It's like I can feel the danger of the island. It's involving me, it's moving me like I've never been moved before. The prison cell has become part of my psyche. It's like everything I've done in my career until now has been complete shit."

Joe looked at Torment and appeared to consider a swift, merciful strike at his head. "Don't be stupid. Why don't you just tell us what happened?"

"Well, unfortunately it involves the lovely Linda who, um, is now very sick."

Joe lifted his head to the heavens. "The lovely Linda."

"I'm afraid so. I would have told you earlier, but she begged me to keep quiet. Apparently her husband is in the Sri Lankan army. The jealous sort. He has a big moustache."

"What happened?"

"Well, that's the strangest thing. Linda has been paying a few visits of late, and, well, one thing led to another. She couldn't understand why I was staying in such a dank sort of place, by the way. In the cell. But that's neither here nor there. Because I understand and I told her it was all for a damn good reason.

"What happened, Chris?"

"Well, we were asleep, but I seem to recall the trap door in the roof opening. Like it was a dream. And then I fell asleep again and I dreamt this man dressed in black – it was too dark to tell who but for some reason I thought it may have been that ghastly Robert Pattinson – crept on to the beam above my bed. From his top pocket he pulled some cotton thread and a phial. He unravelled the cotton so it fell to just above my head. I dreamt that beads of sweat appeared on my forehead as he unscrewed the phial and poured three drops on to the cotton. Drop followed drop down the string. It was just like that Bond film in Japan... What's the matter?"

"You're telling us your dream, Chris," said Joe. "I don't want to hear about your dreams."

"No, but wait. This is the spooky part. I woke up, Joe. I woke up, and I opened my eyes, and what did I see?"

"I don't know. Dolly Parton?"

"I saw the string! The end of it was about two inches above

my nose. And I could see it was wet!"

"Are you trying to tell me they tried to kill you by dabbing your nose with wet string?"

"Don't be silly, Joe. It was that James Bond film, 'You Only Live Twice'. A drop of something reached the bottom of the string and was about to fall..."

"On to your nose."

"Into my mouth, man. But then Linda turned in her sleep and pushed me... actually she kneed me in the balls, and before I could take stock, a drop had fallen into *her* mouth."

I looked at Joe and wondered what he was thinking. Best laid plans of mice and men, etc. As for me, I was thinking: this man Torment is enjoying the attention far too much, but he doesn't deserve to die. But then, is Joe seriously trying to kill him, or is he just playing games?

"Anyway she got the shits," Torment was saying. "Almost immediately. There was poison on that string, man, and that's not the only thing. She pissed off, which was okay with me, and whoever was up in the roof beams, Robert Pattinson or no Robert Pattinson, had pissed off too. I was lying there, wondering what to do, when the next thing I knew, the next thing I felt, was a spider, as big as an omelette, crawling over my elbow. I found out this morning that its bite can kill within seconds, an agonizing death that contorts the victim's features hideously."

"Who told you that?" Joe shanked a four iron.

"One of these sports people." Torment looked around. "They seem to be all over the place. But that's not the point. The spider crawled up on to my face, where it paused, looked around, and sat down on my nose."

All Torment could do was blow at it or shout very loudly. He was staring at it cross-eyed. The spider stood up, stretched, and walked leisurely across Torment's cheek. The moment it left his face, Torment leapt out of bed, put on a shoe, hopped to the other side of the bed, waited for it to climb down to the floor – and stamped.

"As if I hadn't had enough excitement," he said.

"Anyway, you're alive and well, that's the main thing," Joe said.

"No, but I haven't finished."

As Torment was shaving that morning with a cigar clamped between his teeth, out of the corner of his eye, in the mirror, he saw a slim panatela of a snake moving slowly across the floor towards his feet. He recognised it from the guidebook as a species only found on Macho. It was one of the world's most venomous snakes but its bark apparently was even worse than its bite. The world's only barking snake accelerated towards Torment who had seconds to act. His mind moved quickly. Next to the basin was a can of hairspray (ha! what had Joe said about ruling out a James Bond contender who used hairspray?) which Torment lit with the end of his cigar, turning it into a flame thrower which he turned into the face of the snake! The reptile stopped wagging immediately and gave a couple of ferocious woofs that sent shivers down Torment's spine.

"It was a lucky escape," Torment said.

"Very lucky," Joe said. "You were very… intuitive."

"Oh Joe, to explain the freedom I have found since coming to Macho," Torment said as a Sri Lankan pro arrived to give Joe putting tips. "Don't you see? I am paying some sort of penance. It's my karma. These experiences, the narrow escapes, the physical togetherness with the anger of the oppressed, have all served to, well, to harden me, to make a man out of me. Just like you said."

I felt myself nodding off there for a moment.

"I think you have been extraordinarily brave," Joe said.

"Thank you."

"Not a cowardly bone in your body."

"What you reap, you sow."

"Chris, you mean what you sow, you reap."

"In a way, that's true too."

Joe had the putter tight in his grip. Dismissing the pro, he marched back to the house.

I had been brushing up on my tennis. Among the sportsmen on the island were a couple of coaches from the Philippines. They were good players but useless disciplinarians.

"What do you think about my backhand?" I said that evening as the sun went down over Torment's outhouse.

"Please sir, it is not for us to say."

"Well should I put my weight on the front foot or the back?"

"Sir, it is entirely up to you."

I saw Torment leaning against a palm tree.

"That was in, sir," one of the coaches said.

"Way out. Game, set and match to you."

"It was in, sir. We must insist."

"Look, enough." I walked away from the court. "Chris, we have to talk."

"If it's about your sister..."

"No, it's not about my sister."

"Or these bloody Pattinson vampire people..."

"No."

"Maria then..."

"It's not about Maria." I looked around. A 360-degree scowl. There was a camera perched on the wire netting around the tennis court and another two on top of the main house. All were pointed in our direction. Could they pick up what we were saying? Could someone read our lips? I put my hand to my mouth. "Chris, we have to have a private chat."

"Miss Benito has a private jet? I don't understand."

"I'm speaking with my hand over my mouth."

"I can't hear you. You're speaking with your hand over your mouth."

"I'm speaking like this on purpose."

"Again, I can't quite catch what..."

"Look, be quiet." I lifted the front of my shirt to my face as if wiping dust out of my eyes. "Listen to me. I have to tell you something urgently and in private and I don't want these cameras to pick up what I am saying. Do you understand?"

"I understand." Torment lifted a cupped hand to his mouth. "Is Miss Benito a bit of all right?"

"There is no Miss Benito, Chris. Can you get out of your cell tonight?"

"Any time."

"Nine o'clock. In the boathouse."

Joe had been keeping himself much to himself and I had no trouble excusing myself from Waverly and a couple of the other staff, taking a few beers down to the beach. There were explosions on and off all the time now, mostly from the mainland, with a few flashes coming from beyond the horizon. Torment was waiting at the boathouse, uncharacteristically smoking a cigarette. We went inside and I pulled out a small flashlight.

"Chris, we have to be quiet. Things aren't all that they seem."

"What do you mean?"

"You'd better take a look at these." I passed over Joe's pictures and watched Torment's face as he realised what they were. His mouth fell slowly open. He held one of the pictures up to the light, turned it upside down, then craned his neck to the side to look at it the right side up again.

"I'm upside down," he said at last.

"I can see that."

"I'm wearing nothing but a loin cloth."

"That would appear to be the case."

"With a belt around my neck. Why would I do that?"

"I was hoping you could tell me. Joe seems to think it is some sort of auto-erotic asphyxiation."

"But I, I have no idea what that means. Do you mean some sort of *sex game*?"

"Yes."

"Auto-erotic asphyxiation? Breathing in car fumes? That sort of thing?"

"No, no, no."

"Because that just simply isn't me. It sounds disgusting."

"Nothing to do with car fumes. Apparently some people get off on choking their air supply. Don't ask me. So what are you doing exactly?"

"Hadley, you don't get it. When I say that simply isn't me, I mean that... that person in the picture... simply isn't me."

"You've been set up."

"Apparently so. But by whom?"

"I know by whom. Whom by. I know who set you up."

"Who?"

"First off, I had better explain a few things. I have a couple of beers. You want one?"

Torment, a cigarette gripped between his lips, somehow flipped the cap off the bottle with the side of his hand. In the torchlight, he did indeed look tougher.

"What happened to your first movie, 'Great Expectations'? You were Pip, right?"

"It never got made. They were filming in the wrong place. Should have been more marshy. Also, there were a couple of accidents. The director got sick. *I* got sick. Why do you ask?"

"Did you know I was there?"

"I didn't. As a reporter? For the local rag?"

I nodded. "It was the scene where Magwitch gets caught in the marshes. Do you know who else was there?"

"Who?"

"Our friend Joe."

An explosion from the mainland was loud enough to shake the boathouse. Dust fell from the roof beams.

"Joe?"

"He was there in the Fens, monitoring the whole thing. There were American cars, limos, parked away from where all you actors were. You probably don't remember."

"I wasn't there. The Magwitch scene was with the younger Pip. What was Joe doing there?"

"He was doing what he said he does. He's a big mover and shaker, a glorified casting agent. He didn't want that film made. Don't ask me why. He was a big fan of the David Lean version."

"So he caused the accidents? Made me sick? Yeah, right." I said nothing. "You're saying he *did* cause the accidents? He made me sick?"

"It gets worse."

I gave Torment the gist of how I had been recruited, how I had been followed in Hong Kong and probably long before I was ever in Hong Kong, and what Joe's stated aim was. I explained how I had always hated Torment for what he had done to my sister, and most recently for what I had seen of him with Maria and how Joe had rubbed that in my face.

"What did he say I'd done to Maria?"

"He didn't have to say anything. He showed me the movie."

"Oh."

"And I saw you in Joe's flat in Wanchai. That was me peering in the window. You were all over her."

"Oh I see."

"Are you going to tell me nothing happened?"

"Well, that's not quite true."

"What's not true?"

"That nothing happened." I closed my eyes. "You see, I did try it on with her, that night of the junk party. And again when we were at Joe's flat discussing the video…"

"Discussing the video?"

"That's all it was. The video was a put-up job. We made it the next day. I wasn't all over Maria, I was doing what I was being told to do the next day in the video at that god-forsaken bar of yours. It was a rehearsal. The ending was faked. Joe was mad at you, Hadley. That's what I thought then. But now I see it was probably to get you on board to help set *me* up."

"And you tried it on with Maria?"

"I did, I'm afraid."

"But she wouldn't play ball?"

"She wouldn't play anything. Told me to... how did she put it? – eat shit and die. Those were her exact words. How did you know?"

"I didn't know anything."

There were more explosions and the thwump, thwump, thwump sound of a helicopter out at sea.

"Why is he so determined to stop me playing Bond?"

"He told me there's a 'heritage' to protect, but don't ask me how he intends to protect it or who else he has in mind."

"It makes me even more determined."

"For fuck's sake no, Chris. Either he's sane and motivated or he is completely mad, but either way he is dangerous. He set up Chen and obviously he set up the attempts on your life here. I just don't know if they were serious, or if he was just playing. But he has money and power. He can do anything he likes."

"What do we do now then? And how are these Pattinson people involved?"

"Complete mystery. What we do though is I call Shrubs and tell them we need to get out of here. This kind of thing they can do, some sort of medical evacuation, or we get that pompous brigadier back."

"I'd better be going."

"Chris, keep this all to yourself."

"Who is there to tell, except the sports pros and the fitness freaks?"

"Well, don't tell the lovely Linda. When she gets over all the excitement, I mean. She will want an explanation."

"Don't worry, I'll give her more than..."

"Don't say it, Chris. Please."

"Sorry."

I went back to the house and locked on to a satellite signal through the window. I called Baxter.

"Hadley, is that you?"

"Yes, sorry to call so late but it is pretty urgent."

"Are you safe? How did you escape?"

"Escape what?"

"Hadley, the papers are now saying Chris Torment has been taken hostage for real. With you."

"Oh not this again. He *hasn't* been taken hostage. What do you mean 'with me'?"

"Hadley, calm down. You'd better let me read it. *Actor Chris Torment has been taken hostage after surviving a new assassination attempt in Sri Lanka and is being held together with a British journalist he knew at school.*"

I slowly reached across and turned out the ceiling light, not knowing why. I sat down on my bed.

"Hadley, are you there?"

"I'm here, Rodney. Can you tell me the source?"

"Why are you whispering?"

"What's the source?"

"It's this Chen guy. Is he right? Have you both been taken hostage?"

"You mustn't believe everything you read in the newspapers."

"Hadley, why are you whispering? Are you all right? Have you been taken hostage?"

"Not as far as I know. Don't put anything out." I heard a creak in the teak floor outside my room. "Rodney, I'll have to call you back. But I am safe. So far."

I put the phone down and went to the door and knew before I tried it that it would be locked. Then I heard the hissing of the gas from the air-conditioner. They had done this to Patrick Mc-Goohan as John Drake in 'Danger Man'. An undertaker wearing a top hat had come to his door and sprayed something through the letterbox. And when Drake came to, he was suddenly in a new series called 'The Prisoner'. Turned out to be a good career move. Where will I be when I wake up? If I wake up, that is.

The answer turned out to be the boathouse. At first I thought I was dreaming, but the pain in my wrists assured me I was awake. I was pinioned on the ground, held down by the wrists and the ankles. Above me was the wooden roof and cross beams, decked out with assorted telescopic and microscopic instruments, two crossbows, a jar of liquid and yards of wiring. A man, wearing a black diving suit and black eye patch, was standing at the back of a speedboat propped upright on the sand by wooden bollards. Next to him were a pair of oxygen tanks and a speargun.

"And so I am afraid, my dear Mr Bond, death may be slow, but it is certain."

"What are you playing at?" asked Chris Torment. "How did we get here? Who are you?"

I turned my head. True enough, Torment was lying manacled on the ground next to me.

"There is no one here to stop me," the man said. "No one knows where you are, 007, let alone Her Majesty's Secret Service, and I shall be the last to leave the island. Alone. Your friend had the chance to call in the cavalry and he failed."

It was meant to be Emilio Largo, the baddie from 'Thunderball'.

"Welcome back to the land of the living, Mr Leiter." The man was addressing me now. I was Bond's U.S. secret service sidekick, Felix Leiter, it seemed. I raised my head as far as I could.

"Why has Joe put you up to this?" I asked. "What's going on?"

"I see you are confused," the man said. "I have been explaining to Mr Bond how I have to let you both die. Perhaps you would care to assure him that not even the mighty CIA can help."

I tried to collect my thoughts. I remembered the phone call with Baxter. I remembered that the press was saying I had been taken hostage. I remembered the gas coming through the air-conditioner.

"Chris?"

"Oh dear. Perhaps, Mr Bond, you could explain what is happening. The tide, after all, is rising."

Torment turned as far as he could towards me. "The thing is, Felix..."

"Felix?"

"Yes, Felix. You are Felix Leiter, are you not? My trusted friend and CIA agent who always turns up just in time to get me out of all kinds of trouble?" Then in a whisper out the side of his mouth: "Say yes, you bastard. You are Felix Leiter. I am James Bond. This is one of those fucking vampire people, I'm sure of it. He's gone mad."

"He hasn't gone mad," I said. "He's just obeying orders."

"My dear Mr Leiter," the man began. I felt dizzy. "It would appear you are in urgent need of clarification which I am duty bound to provide."

"I want my mum."

"Obviously some sort of clever code, Mr Leiter, but it won't help you now."

"Nurse!"

"As I have explained to Mr Bond, I am about to leave the island but I am afraid it would not help my business interests if I were to allow you to follow." The man, definitely one of the Pattinson people, checked his diver's watch. "It is now 0700 hours. As the sun rises in the sky, it will catch the lens you see in the opening directly above your heads at such an angle, and in exactly seventy-two minutes from now, that beam will be magnified and focused into a laser-thin shaft of light which in turn will activate a solar cell. That cell will activate a switch mechanism which will send a signal down these wires to tell that computer..." Pattinson pointed at a box wedged in the eaves, "...to turn itself on." I tried to catch Chris Torment's eye. Planet Hula-hoop, I wanted to tell him, was in alignment with Planet Fruitcake. "Once the computer is activated, it will decode a pre-sent email which will instruct it to..." Pattinson paused.

"Is there any chance..."

"*Silence*, Mr Bond. The pre-sent email will instruct the computer... to make a beeping noise." I could not stifle a yawn. "I hope I am not boring you, Mr Leiter."

"Sorry. Please go on."

"That noise will in turn activate the spring mechanism which will fire the crossbows aimed at your head."

I found myself drumming my fingers on the sand. This was plainly ridiculous.

"I congratulate you, Largo. You seem to have all bases covered. May I ask one question?"

"Of course. Bear in mind, though, that it may be your last."

"Above your head, within reaching distance, there is a jar of transparent liquid. Can I ask what that will do?"

"That, my dear Mr Leiter, is water. It is for drinking in case I get thirsty."

"I see."

"Can I say something?" said Torment.

"Of course, old Mr Bond. Bear in mind, though..."

"Yes, it may be my last thing I say, I know. But you didn't tell, er, Felix that death may actually be slow."

"My apologies, Mr Leiter. Mr Bond is correct. I am sure it hasn't escaped your notice that we are in the boathouse. The boathouse is on the beach, a hundred yards nearer the sea than it was before. If you are still alive when the tide comes in, you will then surely drown."

"Largo."

"Yes, Mr Leiter?"

"Sun's up. Shouldn't vampires all be in their coffins by now?"

"It is certainly time for me to go."

"Why have you done all this?" Torment asked. "Your acting is awful, by the way. You've got as much chance of becoming James Bond as..." He couldn't think of a name.

Largo, aka Pattinson aka Bob the Builder as far as I knew, strapped on the air tanks and put on his mask. He climbed over the side of the speedboat and mumbled some final words which were unintelligible through the glass.

"Take the mask off," I said. "We can't hear you."

"Take it off!" Torment added as though addressing a stripper. The man fumbled with the strap and took off the mask.

"I said I'm putting on a part. Just wanted to have some fun. Joe said you would like it." He replaced the mask and left the boathouse, fastening the door behind him.

"Lunatic," Torment shouted after him. "Where is Joe? *Loser!*" Another explosion rocked the boathouse, sending dust down from the beams as before. "I am never going on any mercy mission again. I'm never leaving England."

"Do you think this mechanism of his really works?"

"His mechanism is a joke. There's no mainstay for a start."

"Mainstay. That's a good word. You know about this sort of stuff then?"

Torment shrugged his shoulders as much as the manacles allowed. "I'm not completely stupid. The trigger to this device, if there is any device, seems to rely on the sun hitting that glass at a very precise angle. And a bomb has just shaken the whole structure."

"That's good. So we will just drown."

"If he has moved the boathouse nearer the water as he said, then I suspect our hands and feet are pinned down to wood under the sand. He, or they, have had no time to lay cement and I don't see and concrete weights. If the tide does come in, I suspect we will float."

"We will float out to sea in the boathouse with this nice speedboat and not be able to move."

"Hopefully someone will see us."

"I am sure the Sri Lankan air force will see us. Then they can blow us out of the water. Maybe Joe will blow us out of the water."

"The cup is always half empty for you, isn't it, Hadley?"

"What are you talking about? There is no cup."

"You got us into this bloody mess, you find a way out."

"Joe got us into this mess. What about the lovely Linda? Won't she be looking for you?"

"I'm feeling horny."

"Totally inappropriate, given the circumstances. We are manacled to floor of a boathouse with crossbows pointed at our heads. The sun is rising. I reckon we have about half an hour left."

There was a knock on the door. Torment and I shouted "help" in unison.

"Hello, can I come in?"

"Help!"

Whoever it was now was putting an arm to the door. Once, twice, then in he came, rocking all the optical equipment above my head. The jar of water fell and smashed on the prow of the speedboat. I had my eye, unblinking, on the crossbows.

"Hello there," said another Robert Pattinson. "I have no idea what you are up to but it looks groovy. What are you looking at?"

The violence of the entrance had altered the tilt of the boathouse and a narrow, laser-like shaft of sunlight bore down on the solar panel. Torment and I could not take our eyes off the crossbows.

"Vampire man, whoever you are, turn off the computer!" Torment said.

"There's no time to do anything!" I said.

"You mean that thing up there in the roof beams?" This was the second Pattinson. "I can't reach it."

"Turn the fucker off!"

"Perhaps if you had a step-ladder or..."

"It's flashing a red light!"

"Is that some sort of a signal?"

"It's making a clicking noise. Hit those crossbows! They're aimed right at our heads!"

"Well, actually I have a key to unlock you."

"Too late! Listen!"

The computer had logged itself on. It went: "Beep, beep, beep."

"I think I'm going to throw up," Torment said.

"Tell Maria I'm sorry!" I said.

"Hadley, I'm sorry too! Pattinson, tell Maria I'm sorry!"

"Why are you sorry?" I asked. "You said nothing happened."

"Sorry to interrupt," said the look-alike. "It seems the computer has turned itself off again." We looked at the crossbows. All was still. The shaft of light had gone. "The red light has stopped flashing. Actually, I have a key to unlock you. But only if you're ready. I can go away and come back if you like."

"Quick, man, quick. Where did the key come from?"

"It was on the table in the house."

"Along with a little bottle with a label that said 'drink me'?"

"Are you thirsty, Hadley?"

"I am, Chris, as it happens, but actually that was a subtle cross-reference to 'Alice in Wonderland', which right now makes a lot more sense than any of this. Where is Joe?"

"He's gone," the look-alike said, as we rose unsteadily from the floor, stretching our arms and massaging our wrists. "Everyone has gone. Was this little game lots of fun? Joe said it would be lots of fun."

The house was deserted, the outhouse was deserted. Everyone had vanished and the helicopter next to the house had gone. The DVDs had been cleared away, as had the sat-phone and the golf machine. All in a matter of hours. Chris Torment and I hitched a lift back to the mainland with the army.

CHAPTER FOURTEEN

BACK IN HONG KONG, Baxter took me to lunch at a Thai restaurant on the Wanchai strip. I could see the Rawhide Club over the road, shuttered in the shade. The only time I had been this way in daylight was after dawn, when the noise of the trams a block to the south drowned out the sound of expats. I did not call Maria. I had spent an hour composing an email to Baxter to explain what had happened but didn't know what reaction I was going to get.

"Have you seen the papers today?" Baxter began.

"No. Just got up, to tell you the truth."

"Have you heard about your movie being shelved?"

"Shelved?"

"We only did a short piece, but the newspapers have more."

Baxter threw down a copy of the Hong Kong Express. I read:

The curtain went up on Act 3 of the comic drama surrounding the movie 'I Love Hong Kong' on Tuesday, when its exasperated director said its release had been pushed back indefinitely.

"What?"

For those unfamiliar with the story so far, Act 1 had a supposed attempt on the life of the leading actor, Chris Torment, by a Chinese-Sri Lankan separatist group that doesn't exist.

Act 2 detailed the was-he-or-wasn't-he-kidnapped drama in the Sri Lankan war zone amid rumours of strange, if not highly decadent, goings-on on the island of Macho.

Act 3 began with director Adolf Lee saying the release date had been put back for financial reasons, prompting speculation on whether it would be released at all.

"What reason did they give?" Baxter asked.

"Didn't read that far."

I read the caption under an unflattering picture of Adolf Lee with flailing arms.

"Someone appears out to get us," it read.

I found the full quote in the story:

Lee said production was well under way, with the only filming left to do being that of the mist over the Peak now the humidity had arrived.

Then the phone call came from head office in Los Angeles, citing unspecified budgetary problems.

"We have been running under budget. I don't understand," Lee told the Express. "Someone appears to be out to get us. Everyone who has been involved with this, who has seen the rushes, has applauded it. It is a watershed for Chris Torment and Panda Koo."

"This is Joe again," I said.

"Are you sure?"

"I'm not sure about anything. But he has the power. If Chris is as good as they say, then it all makes sense."

Baxter studied the menu. "I don't know if you have had time to read your emails, but the bosses in London are very grateful that you, how shall I put it, kept your head out there."

"That's nice to hear."

"They feel that Shrubs came out of this looking good, with many other agencies and papers picking up on the rumours and pictures. Even the Chen guy you managed to knock down as a story.

"But they did wonder if you could have made more of the sense of this guy holding you both against your will."

"But we weren't, Rodney. The source for that story, this guy Chen, was a stooge as you say. He was put up to the so-called assassination attempt."

"Set up by Joe?"

"Yes." I sat back in my chair.

"And we know next to nothing about Joe."

I sighed. "I met him years ago, on my first paper, as I have said. The person who knows most about him is probably Panda Koo."

"The Cantonese girl?"

"The actress, yes. She is under Joe's direct control and will never say anything against him."

"So tell me again. I have to get it clear for London: you say that this man, Joe Stein, is a big noise in the movie world, but that no one has really heard of him?"

"I am afraid so, yes."

"No one can find his name or his company online."

"Correct."

"Yet he has been tracking you, on and off, since you first started out in this business."

"It's possible."

"And his over-riding concern is stopping Chris Torment from becoming James Bond."

I opened my palms on the table, as if to say: I know it sounds crazy, but that's about it.

"So he re-introduces himself to you in Hong Kong, fills your head with lots of bad things about your school buddy…"

"He wasn't my school buddy."

"…and asks you to help ruin his reputation."

"I made clear I wouldn't do anything unethical. That's as much as I had said when you sent me off to Sri Lanka with him, which, as it happens, came a day after he had suggested the idea to me."

"I hope to God you're not suggesting we're involved in this little charade as well."

"Of course not."

"Let's stay with what we know for now. I want to be able to write it down in chronological order. With bullet points. You go to Sri Lanka, to Jaffna."

"Yes."

"Then the brigadier takes you off in a helicopter, away from the press crew, with Torment."

"He said it was Shrubs's idea. It also made sense, as we were trying to track down the Chinese group."

"Which doesn't exist."

"Exactly. Even the brigadier suspected as much."

"I'll come to that. Joe turns up at a hotel during a Robert Pattinson look-alike competition at *another* hotel, causes a lot of explosions, wrecks the hotel and whisks you and Torment off to another island."

"I know it sounds implausible."

"Don't stop me, I'm on a roll. On the island, he tells Torment he wants to toughen him up to help him become the next Bond. Torment says terrific. Exit Torment to some sort of cell. Then stories start appearing saying Torment has been kidnapped, there are attempts on his life, then pictures arrive of Torment in some sort of automobile sex game..."

"No automobiles."

"...You write a couple of stories saying he hasn't been kidnapped and then you *yourself* get kidnapped..."

"Well, that's debatable. I got tied down in a boathouse with Chris. It was a game. Joe had wanted me to write lies; to make out Chris was gay, or something like that, to smear him."

"...and get tied up in a boat shed with a crossbow aimed at your head. Then..." Baxter paused for a drink of water. "...then one of these Robert Pattinson people turns up with a key to save you."

"That's true. A Robert Pattinson clone."

"One of his clones. I see. And then a computer goes beep."

"The computer went beep before we were saved."

"But absolutely nothing happened. And perhaps the weirdest part of the story is that your chum Chris Torment can corroborate this."

"Yes. Certainly the last bit."

Baxter stared at me. First into my left eye, then my right.

"Shall we have a drink?"

"Sure."

"A beer?"

"Thanks."

"Waiter, a San Mig and a double Scotch." Baxter turned back to me. "Barring the possibility that this is all a crock of shit, could it be that you may have stumbled on to a huge story?"

"It could. And I am the only one with it. But I'm not sure we could ever write it. Joe wouldn't let us."

"Could it also be that, before all these extraordinary things started to happen, you could have established that there was no such thing as the Chinese liberation group with the silly name?"

"We all tried. We had Chen; we had people talking about the group. We couldn't just ignore them."

"It was a hoax. There's a learning curve here. About how not to fall for a hoax. If we have a drill, we must reinforce it. You can give a course. What has happened to Joe now? Is he in a secure asylum?"

"Again, we don't know. He cleaned up thoroughly before he left. He had a helicopter on the island which had gone when we were released."

"But we know what happened to Chen."

"Afraid not."

"No, I am telling you. We know what happened to him. All charges have been dropped. Not even done for wasting police time. He has powerful friends."

"Obviously."

"He was last seen heading to a restaurant down the road with a bunch of his mates. He was laughing at the time."

"Laughing all the way to the banquet."

"Nice."

"I've used it before."

"Doesn't matter." Baxter knocked his drink back in one. "The punter doesn't know."

BAXTER TOLD me to take a couple of weeks off. Shrubs had holiday homes dotted around the outlying islands for visiting executives. I was to take a psychological evaluation and could choose a retreat free of charge.

"Take a girlfriend," Baxter added.

I hadn't seen Maria since my visit to Joe's Rich Mansion. I sat at my usual seat in the Honest Bar and waited to see her turn and react. I was ready to punish her for that intimate scene in the penthouse apartment when I knew that she had done nothing underhand.

Maria turned. The look on her face was undisguised joy. She poured a beer and placed it softly in front of me.

"What's the matter?" she asked.

"What happened with you and Chris?"

"He bar-fined me, Hadley. Why are you angry? He also bar-fined me last night."

"Last night?"

"He was very sad because his movie isn't going well. He wanted to say goodbye."

"What?"

"He was very unhappy. They stopped his film. Your film."

"Is he leaving Hong Kong?"

"I don't know."

What else don't you know? What else don't you want to tell me? I went outside, lit a cigarette and called Torment.

"I'm furious," Torment said. "You can't tell me it's not connected with what went on on that island. What a waste of my time. I'm going to fix him."

"Don't even think about it."

"Why not? He's not all powerful."

Oh, that's okay then. "What are you going to do?" I asked.

"I fly to London tomorrow. To try to find out what's going on with this film. Then, I have no idea."

"I hope you have dropped any idea of becoming James Bond." Silence at the end of the phone.

I went back inside and told Maria about the retreat I had chosen on Cheung Chau, a small, sleepy island the shape of a strangled duck with a bustling harbour packed full of fishing junks and seafood restaurants.

"They want me to get over all this, take a couple of weeks off. Come back to work fresh. What do you think?"

"Will you let me come?"

"Of course."

The Shrubs holiday home was a third-floor, two-bedroom apartment overlooking the ferry pier and facing west, a McDonald's a one-minute walk to the south. The sun was setting over the blue hills of Lantau, a much bigger, rural island which was home to a giant bronze Buddha and a hill-top Trappist Monastery which raised dairy cows and where no one spoke a word. I could see planes lining up to land at Chek Lap Kok airport, itself built from the remains of a demolished island. Three white lights all in a row, like wasps returning to their nest. Trappists, I thought. So when the cow kicks over the chief monk's bucket full to the brim with milk, he doesn't say something short and appropriate like "fuck"? It may be in Latin, but he definitely says it.

I hired a dilapidated junk, its wet, wooden deck awash with ropes, lanterns, nets, beams and other joists of seasoned hard wood with maritime names I did not know. Three Barbie dolls wobbled from a line of bare electric bulbs as a gas stove hissed furiously in the stern, drowning out the sound of the diesel engine on a warm and muggy night. Two old women were cooking steamed fish, steamed prawns and minced pigeon. One told the other twice to fuck her mother, which made everyone laugh, including the captain, a cigarette clenched between his teeth, and even Maria. *Diu nei lou mou,* Cantonese for 'fuck your old mother', is so common in some Hong Kong circles that it is almost a courtesy.

The junk set off in the direction of Hong Kong. Maria and I ate as lights twinkled from Lamma Island, home to assorted gweilo families, hippies and journalists. Including Rupert the sub who was probably sitting in front of his television set right then, staring at the ceiling and shaking his legs. Smaller junks appeared and old Hakka women in broad-rimmed hats screamed words of greeting, their cackles fading as the boats passed. The cooks told them all to fuck their mothers.

"I hope your meal is to your satisfaction?"

I didn't have to turn. I looked up at Maria who was looking above and behind my head at Joe, the frown replaced by a half smile. "*Diu nei lou mou,*" she said softly.

"Hello my dear." Joe walked slowly to the table, sat down next to Maria, took her hand and kissed it. "As always, you look remarkable."

Maria did look remarkable. She also looked remarkably... complicit. Snap out of it, I told myself.

"So they've given you some time off?" Joe asked me. "To get over you ordeal?"

He was wearing a striped black-and-white t-shirt, like a nineteenth century prisoner, his hair wet and swept back and hanging loose like he had just had a shower. A backpack hung from his shoulder. I pointed a finger in his face, wondering where he had come from, where he was going, and whether or not this was his boat.

"What do you want with me?" I said. "What are you *doing* here?"

"Questions, questions. Do you know the way to San Jose? Remember that one? I've come to say adios."

I sat, exhausted. "Whatever you are doing, you are going to get caught. My bosses know, everyone knows. You can't play with people's lives."

Joe was staring at Maria. Like a magician waiting for someone to appreciate a trick. What trick? "I've come to say it's all over."

"What's all over?" I asked.

"My job. Here in Hong Kong."

"You mean Chris?"

"Yup. Done and dusted. Danger no longer clear and present. Franchise safe and in good hands." Joe was still looking at Maria.

"Just like that? They don't want him, so your job is over?"

"Just like that."

"Where have you come from?" Maria asked softly. Like an ex-lover.

"Downstairs. Sorry, below decks. Afore decks. The front."

"Why did you stop the Hong Kong film?" I asked.

"You are jumping to conclusions again. That film is a work of art. Your Chris Torment does a pretty good job. People will get to see it eventually."

"Who will be the next James Bond?"

"I can't tell you that. But I can tell you it ain't going to be your buddy. Too much baggage."

"How do you know...?"

"You're ready to jump to a conclusion again. You see Maria naked with another woman in my apartment and anybody and everybody is convicted of a crime."

"I didn't see Maria naked with another woman."

"My bad." Joe put his hand in front of his mouth. Maria suppressed a giggle. Joe put his hand on her knee.

"What the fuck's been going on?" I asked.

"Boy oh boy, Hadley, it's like pushing buttons. Just give it a rest."

Joe pulled his bag on to the table and felt inside. I worried for a moment that he was going to pull out a gun.

"I have something for you, Hadley, but that can wait. Something else here is more important. Now where did I put it?" He searched through the bag. "That vessel behind me, by the way, approaching at speed, I believe is the police. Asia's finest. Here it is." Joe pulled out a pair of goggles attached to a white contraption that looked like a gasmask. He chuckled. "You both look so worried. I wanted to show you this. This is a working model of those neat little underwater breathing devices used in 'Thunderball'."

"The police are coming for you, Joe."

"Let them come. At the time, a snorkel like this was just make-believe. But with today's technology, anything is possible. I ran this one up myself."

A search light picked out the junk and a siren gave a brief whelp. Joe grabbed Maria and me by the arms. "Not a word more to anyone about any of this. Do you understand? Not a word." The police launch approached. "You know my ways. No Magwitch caught in the marshes for me. Be good."

And with that he strode back to the galley. The police boat pressed against the side of the junk with a sigh of four outboard motors, pushing the vessel a foot to the side, against its natural course, as woks and bowls clattered to the deck in the stern.

"*Diu nei lou mou*," I heard from the back. It sounded like Joe.

I saw green and red lights on black instruments flashing around the deck of the police launch. Three Chinese officers, wearing their summer olive green uniforms instead of the royal winter blue, clambered nimbly aboard, followed by a bald gwei-lo wearing a pistol at his hip.

"Which one of you is Joe Stein?" the gweilo asked in broad Glaswegian.

"He was here just a second ago," I said. Maria put her hand through my arm. "He may be below deck."

"Check downstairs," the gweilo told his officers.

The policeman, with a sunken face and a tiny white scar on the end of his nose, approached the table and picked up Joe's black bag.

"This man has been a bit of menace, we understand. Does this bag belong to him?"

"It does."

The Chinese officers came back. "Nothing, sir."

"Turn the lights on the water. He can't have got far. Did he jump?"

"He went to the back of the boat," Maria said. "That is all we know."

"How long ago? Seconds? Minutes?"

"Minutes, I suppose," I said. "He's an incredibly resourceful man. I suspect he has escaped."

"Sounds like you want him to escape. That water's bloody cold. What's he left in this bag, then?"

The gweilo turned the bag upside down and out tumbled something gift-wrapped, something pink and a half-eaten sandwich.

"What would a grown man want with a lady's compact?" the policeman asked.

"Can I take a look?"

The gweilo handed over an exact replica of Suzie's pink compact, the one that had clattered to the street in Wanchai. On the silver back was the inscription: *To our darling Suzie on her graduation, from her proud and loving parents*.

"And what's all this then?" the gweilo asked. "It's a present marked 'for your eyes only'. Whose eyes would those be?"

The officer handed it to me. "Seen anything?" he shouted back to his boat.

"Nothing so far, sir."

I unwrapped the gift and frowned. For my eyes only. It was a paperback map of California with a ringed spine.

"Is that where he's from then? California? Could that be where he's going?"

"I don't know."

I looked inside the front cover where there was another inscription.

"*The missing first and last piece of the jigsaw puzzle,*" it read. It was signed Joe.

"What does that mean?" asked the officer, who was standing next to Maria now, looking over my shoulder.

I flicked through the pages, and there, ringed in red, was the answer.

"It's a bit of a private joke," I said. "It has been for years. He's showing me the way to San Jose."